After the Dust Settles

E. J. Astorga

After the Dust Settles is a work of fiction; it is the creation of the author's imagination. If any incidents or events mentioned resemble any true events, it is purely coincidental.

CLF Publishing, LLC.
9161 Sierra Ave, Ste. 203C
Fontana, CA 92335
www.clfpublishing.org

Cover Design by Senir Design. Contact information-info@senirdesign.com.

ISBN 978-1-945102-08-0

Printed in the United States of America.

Dedications

This book is dedicated to my father. Dad, you told me if I work hard enough, and if I ever finish writing an ending (which I knew it took me forever, Dad), I can end up being a writer. But, I think I was a writer the whole time, since birth maybe, and you were just waiting until *I* finally came to that conclusion. So, here it is now- my first book ever. Thank you, Dad. Thank you for believing in me this whole time.

Acknowledgements

I want to thank everyone who made this possible: my family, my friends, especially Val, my partner in crime Ernesto Meza, and above all, Dr. Elliott for taking a chance with me and helping me achieve this dream.

The Light in the Sky

I looked down at my crumbled piece of paper and read what was written, *Dear Dad...* That was it. That's all I had written down. After struggling all night and this morning, barely getting a wink of sleep, this is all I could come up with?

Leaning back on my chair, I blew out air and ran my hands down my face in frustration. I looked out the window to the apartment complex across from me. My dreams were right there. No matter how incredibly sappy that sounded, though I dare not tell anyone for fear of letting them know how sappy it is, I just wanted what was right across from me. There was a nice family right over there, just out of reach. I sometimes snuck a quick glance, when they would leave their window open, seeing them all together sitting down around the kitchen table.

I always envied them, a happy family with a mother, a father, two sons, and a daughter. I wished I had a family like that. A whole family, not just an only child with divorced parents, who was miserable and lonely, no matter how much I had. What I wanted was not physical. What I wanted was something else. Something that everyone takes for granted. What I wanted was to have, no be, a family again.

Well, one parent now. My thoughts started to linger to that eventful day when my parents told me. Once they had sat me down at the head of the table and told me their news, I didn't know what to think. All I felt was rage and sadness that lingered for so many years. I was angry for a very long time after that, but I got better with some help from friends, though I doubt they really did anything, except fuel the fire burning through me. My mother tried to get me to therapy, but talking to a complete stranger who was going to end up telling my mom and dad was unsettling.

My thoughts are my own and who I shared them with was my choice. After a while, I even started to enjoy going from one place to another, having best friends in two big cities, getting twice as many gifts for Christmas and my birthday, even on non-special occasions, just a surprise gift. Both my parents would try to outdo the other. It was fun, as I started to get away with stuff too. I only had to mention what the other allowed me to do. I know I was taking advantage of them, but at the time, I didn't care. They worked long hours, and I barely saw them. So, they would give me all these things. After a while, I figured out they were buying my love. That's when I started noticing more things around me.

Some of my friends with divorced parents said that the gifts were the best part. They went to places with one parent then the other, from amusement parks, concerts and plenty of other fun adventurous places. Those were the best and happiest times of their lives. Without their parents though, it would occasionally be a friend or relative. I know everyone says they would rather be with friends at that age, but honestly, we all want to be with our parents occasionally. We are more comfortable with them because they are our first friends. None of them ever told me how miserable, how lonely, how...sad all of this was.

Then, the blame game started. I could see it in their eyes, just as they could see it in my eyes, too. All the smiles around our parents and friends were just a façade deep down. My friends and I just knew the divorce was our entire fault. I figured that's why I was so angry, but it is who I am now.

"It is not your fault, sweetie. None of this has anything to do with you. We just fell out of love. There's nothing left for us both...but Johnny, we still love you." I remember when my mother and father said that to me. My mother was in tears, and my father had a hard look that showed no emotion. I had never been told the biggest lie ever.

This isn't your fault kept going through my head for a long time after that. Soon, I just learned to accept it. *It was my fault. Maybe I was selfish or...or something. Maybe I ruined their relationship. Did they even want a kid or was I too much to handle?* My mother had to quit going to school, and my dad had to work overtime, but he was able to succeed. My mother took up drinking for a bit...well, they both did. *I guess to drown me out.* The house I grew up in was my haven, as my mom would drink and work on the computer. My dad was never around; he was always busy, but there were times when we would all be together.

Those were the fondest memories. Now, I am here- though with only sad memories.

When we all did split up, I did things I am not proud of, just so I could get attention. I had hoped that would work, but then my dad stopped asking for days to see me, and my mother was all too happy to have me...until she wasn't, and I was just there in the background. I had been stealing, getting drunk, fighting, yelling at my mom, teachers and any adult figure, and now, I am here in front of this paper running away. Just thinking about what to put down next. *I'm being selfish again. That's all I ever am. That's all I'll ever be now.*

Just one paper. Just one paper explaining why I'm going away, I thought as I ran my hands through my hair, while closing my eyes in frustration. I slumped down, and my forehead came crashing down, slamming on the table, hitting the paper and pencil.

"Ouch!" I jumped up quickly, knocking my chair to the ground, as I looked at my reflection in the black screen of my desktop. A long red indentation on my forehead showed the Number 2 pencil nicely etched into my skin.

As I rubbed it and laughed at my own stupidity, a slight vibration came from my phone. Reaching over to unplug it from my charger, I saw whom the call was from. The very same person who I was writing to, but instead of calling, he just sent a text. *Probably too busy for a call anyway.* I guess I couldn't really blame him. *He is a scientist for... something I never bothered remembering.*

"Hey there, Johnny. I know you're in class right now, but when school is over can you come by the lab? I'll let security know. I want to have a talk with you." I was getting ready to make a reply but then thought better of it. I wanted to let him know there would no longer be any more replies. Not ever again.

I reached down and picked up the chair and looked over at the piece of paper. I sighed and walked towards the window. Looking out again at the window across the street from me, I saw the father had arrived home, and he had opened a bottle of wine and had served two cups. I narrowed my eyes and looked at the unknown woman sitting beside him. They clinked glasses and sipped wine, then kissed. I sighed and closed the curtains. I guess families aren't what they used to be. *They are all lies now.*

Sitting back down on my chair, I picked up my pencil and began to write. Looking up at the clock, twenty minutes had gone by, and I was finished. Strangely enough though, I didn't know what I wrote. Everything went by as a blur.

'Dear Dad," I began reading, just as my phone vibrated again, as I got a text from one of my friends at school: "Johnny, where are you? Don't tell me you're ditching because if you are you're a jerk for not giving me an invite." Smiling, I made a quick response and looked down at the paper. With my smile dropping, I texted my friend another quick text, with the same words as the last ones on the letter.

"Goodbye," I said aloud sending the text.

I threw out the contents of my school bag and stuffed it with my most precious possessions, which was hard to decide because I honestly didn't care for much. So a few clothes, toothbrush and toothpaste, and a stack of money from selling most of the gifts my parents had bought me. I zipped it up and walked out my door, but I ran back in as a sudden thought passed through my head.

"Where is it? Where is it?" I asked frantically. I went through my drawers and desk looking and looking for that one picture. My favorite picture of when I was younger, one of the last ones of my mother, father and me. We were smiling and laughing, as they swung me with their arms. I'm not sure who took the picture, but the way they captured that perfect moment, that perfect spot in time had always made me smile. It was my favorite picture and now... now, I couldn't find it anywhere. After a while, I noticed my room looked like a tornado had swept through.

I guess it's for the best, I thought. Nothing to remind me, nothing to make me come back because I had nothing to keep me there anymore.

Once again stepping out of my room, I walked out. Not looking back, I kept walking. Closing the door to my dad's apartment, I kept walking. Down the elevator that seemed to take forever as I was on one of the top floors, and out of the massive lobby, my mindset to never go back, I kept walking, as I went through the revolving doors. Out on the streets, I took a deep breath and willed myself to not look back.

"Hey, kid," a large police officer right behind me said. "Shouldn't you be in school?" he asked with a southern accent.

"Home schooled, sir. I'm heading to the library," I quickly said, lying through my teeth and ending my last words with a smile.

"Alright. Good to hear," he said smiling. "Remember, stay in... umm," he scratched his head and thought of his next words slowly. I gave him a hurried look, pretending that I was in a hurry. "Stay away from drugs, alright," he said frowning at me.

"Yes, sir. Of course. Now if you'll excuse me; economics isn't going to learn itself," I said with a bit of sarcasm and smiled turning around, making a terrified face. As my eyes opened widely, I quickly walked away. After I rounded the corner of a building, I laughed. That was scary and funny, but I made it easily.

Okay, so far so good. I just walked, enjoying the city view and the nice cars here and there. Oh, and nice girls, too! Phew, couldn't forget about them. However, what I absolutely loved and what always captured my attention were the buildings. I loved architecture. An architect is what I really wanted to be, but with my grades, I'd never make it. As I walked, I loved looking up and seeing the beautiful detail and the framework of every building.

Then, I was three miles away from home and further away from school. Luckily, the cop was the first and only one to ask about school. I headed to a bus stop and pulled out some change from my back pocket. I slid that money into my front shirt pocket and looked around me at the busy street I was on. Just one bus to the out-of-state bus stations and then to wherever I wanted. I think I'll go to...I actually don't know where to go. I'll just find out when I'm there.

It was a casual morning, with traffic from one side to the other. Traffic lights flicked red, yellow, and green. Fumes came from sewer grates. With the screeching of a subway, a hoard of people came piling outwards from the subway entrance and exits. Shops advertised their merchandise of clothes, toys, coffee, or food. People walked around, and there were a few other kids by themselves or with families also going from one place to another. It was just another normal day in another city.

I was not familiar with that side of the city, but I loved how busy it was. Being surrounded by people made me feel comfortable. I felt as though I was not as alone as I felt. It reminded me of sardines, and as much as I hate the smell of fish, I liked being packed inside... *Okay, now I'm losing it. I think I'm getting too nervous. Stop, Johnny. Stop. You can't back out now.* I felt myself frowning, as I looked all around me.

I reached the bus stop and leaned against the side frame. Reaching into my pocket, I pulled out my phone and earphones. Plugging them in, I shuffled through my music. My thumb lingered on the play button, as hundreds of thoughts hit my brain, bouncing from one place to another.

"Where am I going?" I looked around me and saw all those strange people. "What will I do once I get there...where is *there* anyway?" My mind wondered off to my mother. *I want to go home*, I thought. I slowly felt myself slide to the ground, with tears slowly flowing down my eyes.

"I miss my mom," I mumbled to myself. "I wish I was back with her. I wish the accident had never happened that she never had to go away. I wish for so much right now." I felt myself shiver as I leaned there, tearing up a bit.

All of a sudden, a blinding white light appeared in the middle of the sky. I quickly got up and stared, as everyone else did, too. Shielding my eyes away from the sudden strong brightness, I felt a force so strong that it pulled the air from my lungs and pulled my phone from my hands. The force was so strong; it pushed me backwards. I felt myself being weightless, and my body left the ground. I was thrown into the air, and I soared backwards, at least a few feet, but luckily, I had a soft landing. As I was pushed into someone, I heard the sharp intake of air from the person behind me. Everything was so bright, and there was no sound from the cars or people for a few seconds, just the rush of the wind. Then, I couldn't see anything, and I couldn't hear anything. Everything went black.

Wake up.

Finally waking up, my eyes were very groggy, and my ears were ringing loudly. Then, they just stopped. Everything was then muffled. I couldn't focus on anything for a few seconds. I wanted to just close my eyes, but I had to focus. When my eyes adjusted and my hearing returned, I only wished it had never come back. I wished my eyes were closed forever because the horrors I saw broke me even more than I was. I felt myself whimper, as I wished I were home right then. What I saw and heard changed my whole concept of life, and I'm sure for everyone, every single person who was there, too.

Windows were broken and glass was raining down. Cars were flipped over on their sides or upside down. Buildings were on fire or in the midst of explosions. Buildings were toppling in on themselves or snapping in half and falling onto the streets or other buildings. There were loud booms and crashes echoing everywhere. The most frightening though was the people; the people on the streets, sidewalks, inside the cars, running out of buildings, through fires, or hanging and falling from the buildings were all screaming and crying. Everything still sounded muffled, but I wanted it that way. I didn't want to hear any of that.

Blood was everywhere.

Suddenly, I saw a small plane crashing into the side of a small skyscraper in the distance, falling in on itself. The force of it brought another building down and both of them went tumbling down. Luckily, I wasn't near it, not even a mile close, but I still felt the heavy rumble through the ground. That was all sudden and terrifying, and I didn't know what to do. Still on the ground, I stared at everything. My eyes were taking everything in, but my mind had difficulty processing the chaos.

Like a bursting dam, my hearing returned, and I was shaking and crying from all that I had heard. Alarms blared from stores, as windows blew inwards from cars that had been pushed inside, and as the smoke cleared, my vision was accompanied by screaming, screeching, and yelling from the people all in pain.

"Help me! Help me!" a woman screamed, from her upside down car. She was thrashing around, trying to free herself.

"Ah!" A sudden scream from across the street erupted into more screams, as a man came running out a burning building, followed by more people all on fire, screeching in pain and agony, running in every direction. Some stumbled and crashed face down onto the streets. Everywhere there were cries for help, for any of their loved ones, hugging, holding, screaming and screeching their names.

I saw a woman hugging a small bundle in her arms, and a small lifeless baby's arm was hanging out of it, with blood seeping from the bottom of the bundle. The blood soaked onto the crying woman. But wait! The baby moved! Then, it started to cry, mixing in with everyone else's cries. The woman just fell backwards. It was she that was bleeding and still was as the blood started to form a small puddle. Then, she fell from the edge of the sidewalk and into the street gutters.

There was an upturned bus, beside the woman's body, that was halfway into a supermarket with no one moving that I could see. I caught sight of the thick black smoke swirling upwards, rising from cars and buildings. Turning my head to my right, directly beside me was a bald man, with a soft blue shirt, the same color as his lifeless eyes that were staring right at me. The rest of his body, below the waist, was under a collapsed building. Rubble rolled down, with some hitting me as it came down.

"Please," I choked out, wanting him to close his eyes to look away from me. Then, the flow of blood started forming all around him, reaching me and coating my hand. I couldn't move. I wanted to jump up and run and keep running, but I couldn't move. I just kept staring at him, as he stared right back at me. Crying and crying right then, I couldn't do anything. People needed help, but I... I just couldn't do anything.

An explosion finally made me turn my attention from the man to my left towards the west, where the skyscraper came down. There were huge columns of dust and dirt rising from that direction. No from every direction- all coming towards me. I could hear the screams getting louder as the dust started to cover everything and everyone- even me. But, I could still vaguely see around me. The dust hadn't gotten too thick at the moment. It was happening all so fast.

I saw an older couple holding each other and a little girl screaming for her mother and father. A delivery truck was on top of a car, and a man on fire dropped down, knees first, landing with a thud near the lifeless woman with the baby. A woman was clutching her purse while sitting on the ground, with a big bloody gash on her leg, gasping for air with her eyes wide, darting quickly left and right. There was a man limping away from the supermarket, holding his arm, which was bloody and dripping down from the fingertips, leaving a small trail from one of the bus windows. The dust engulfed them all, making them fade away.

A piercing siren suddenly rang from behind me, as the windows burst outwards with flames flying outward as if to escape even from themselves. They finally settled into a large roaring fire inside the building. The heat made me feel like I could catch on fire any moment. I could only imagine the murderous fires that would be raging throughout the city, as firefighters would have to go through the disaster and over all the rubble to get to the people. That's if the water hydrants had any more water. That was the fiery inferno of hell everyone talked about. It was more gruesome than anyone could have ever imagined.

As if to answer my wondering thoughts about the fire hydrants, one of them, which was half buried in the rubble beside me, erupted spraying water upwards, as if to escape all the insanity, like I should have been doing right then to escape from it all, but ultimately the water fell back to earth, showering everything and everyone, dead or alive, while containing a bit of the fire behind me.

Then, the thickness of the dust finally settled around me, as I was engulfed in a thick brown curtain and was only grateful, as I didn't have to see any more horrors. I was only forced to listen to the gut-wrenching horrors.

****

I woke up with a few strands of hair and the taste of blood in my mouth. My arms, legs, and head were hanging to my right, as a seatbelt held me in place. I was in the backseat behind the driver's side and...and oh, my God- the car. The car was on its right side. I could see my bag just lying on the window. I fumbled for the seatbelt, and without thinking, I unclipped it. Right away, I knew what a dumb mistake I had made. I hit the bottom of the right door frame, with a thud. The air escaped my lungs. I gasped for air, clutching the roof of the car, clawing at it, as my chest rose, trying to get some air. Suddenly, I remembered what had happened.

I was with my brother Paulo, and we were running very late for my first day at school.

"Lupita!" Paulo had yelled, tapping his foot and leaning with his keys at the front door. "Your butt needed to be downstairs and in that car two hours ago."

"I'm coming! I'm coming!" I had yelled back. "If you would have woken me up two hours ago, I would have been up and ready!" I ran from the bathroom across the hallway and into my room, stuffing my schoolbag with the textbooks. Then, I added some of my "free time" books. *I'm a big book worm,* I thought, as my bag was bulging. *Okay, take some out.... Nah, I'll suffer through it.* I giggled at the idea of the new girl with a bag full of books, arriving late to the class. Then, I frowned *...okay, taking them out now.*

"Don't you start now. I just got back from work! I thought you were going to take the bus." My brother interrupted my thoughts.

"Well, I didn't as you can see." I popped my head from the doorway and rolled my eyes sticking my tongue out.

"Just go get ready!" he yelled.

I quickly ducked back inside, scared at his sudden outburst. I ran over to my bed and reached for a sweater then ran back. I again quickly ran to the bathroom, as I threw the sweater at his face. "Ha-ha, you jerk!"

"Lupita! Get ready already!"

"One second!" I reached for a comb and buried it into my hair, saving the brushing for when I got in the car. I applied some makeup when suddenly, my brother showed up in the doorframe, taking up the whole space with his tall built figure. He looked at me, with his eyebrows set in a scowl.

"What?" I asked. "I need to put my makeup on."

"Oh my God, Lupita! Now! Now! Now!" he yelled again.

"Mi dios," I gasped, with one hand over my heart. "When did we become Mister Grouchy Pants?"

"Lupita," he hissed between his teeth.

I ran past him, grabbing my bag and running to the front door. "Hurry up! I don't have all day!" I giggled, as I ran down the apartment stairs and onto the sidewalk.

I heard my brother's loud footsteps, as he ran behind me the whole time, so I knew not to slow down for him. I heard the jingle of the car keys as he unlocked his small car, and I yanked open the back door and threw my stuff inside.

"Hurry up! We are very late," he said ducking my head and pushing me inside the car.

"Touchy, touchy," I tisked at him, as he slid into the driver's seat and started the car. "I don't like being touched by the way." My hands were flying with the comb as they quickly combed my hair.

"Okay listen, Lupita." He turned around to look at me with a serious expression. That was the time I knew I needed to shut up and behave because he was being serious, and it pertained to both of us. "I need you to be on time for tomorrow and the next few days. I can't have you being late. It will affect both of us... and then, if it gets too bad, you won't be able to stay with me."

I sighed and nodded, "Yea, I understand." I couldn't mess up at that point. I was only sixteen, and the state would take me away. *They had threatened me with that last time before my brother came to get me.* I could always go live with Mom... if our grandparents would let us, and they probably wouldn't. They didn't like our father, as if we did, and they didn't like us. My head was starting to hurt just thinking about it. It had been a big drama fiasco, and so, we were all separated.

"Alright then. Let's get this show on the road now." He started to steer out. Then, he quickly slammed on the brakes, making me hit my head on the back of his seat. The car behind us blared the horn. "Watch where you're going," he yelled, rolling down the window and cursing under his breath.

"Ouch," I said sarcastically, smiling and tapping my head, as I met his narrowed eyes in the rear view mirror.

"Do not make me turn this car around, young lady," he said through clenched teeth. I inched forward, so I could whisper in his ear. I said, "Ouch," just as he turned around and lunged at me. I quickly pulled myself back and giggled, as his seat belt restrained him.

"Come on!" The man in the car behind us stuck his head out his car and yelled at us, as he blared his horn again, followed by more car horns behind him.

"Paulo, we're going to be late," my voice stern and serious now. He tapped his fingers on the steering wheel and breathed out.

"That's it, bro. Deep breaths in." I sucked in as much air as I could. "And out," and I let out air emphasizing my words.

He pulled out, and then, hit the road going forward, finally earning the end of the honking horns. "Sometimes, Lupita. I wonder whom you take after," he said smiling and shaking his head. "But, I think you are in your own little world."

I smiled and looked out the window, as we stopped at a red light. *My own world,* I thought. *Wait,* my mind did a mental stop, and I turned to look at him scowling. "Is that supposed to be a fat joke?"

He just burst out laughing and laughing. He couldn't stop, even after we hit the next set of lights, and because laughter is contagious, I laughed too. Tears were streaming down my face, as I hugged my body from the pain in my stomach. But, it soon died down, and we both wiped away the tears and just remained silent but smiling.

After a while, I noticed we weren't going to the school. We were going in the opposite direction. "Hey, Paulo? You do know that my school is the other way, right?"

"What?" he yelled out quickly, turning the signal lights to make a U-turn at the next stop. "Why didn't you tell me that before?" He angrily gripped the steering wheel with both hands.

"I thought you knew where it was at," I stated flatly.

"Clearly, I don't," he groaned, putting his head on the steering wheel.

"Relax, it's my first day. What else could go wrong?"

"Lupita, please. Right now is not the time for jokes." The light had turned green, and he made the U-turn making his way back towards home.

"Well, it wasn't even my fault to begin with."

"Just tell me where it is okay! It's three blocks this way right?" He pointed forward with an outstretched hand. "And yes, it was Lupita. If you had just..." a sudden bright light stopped him from finishing the rest of his thoughts.

I looked out my window, as suddenly the car behind us slammed into us, and my whole body went forward, and like a whiplash, my head came back making a "pop" noise. Then, it felt as if someone lifted the car up into the air and threw us higher up then backwards several times. I felt more; then, I saw my hair slapping my face and glass hitting and slicing my face and arms, wherever my skin was exposed. Then, darkness.

On the doorframe, now on the ground, groaning and coughing, I looked up to my brother's seat, and it was empty. I leaned over, the palms of my hands on glass, digging into my flesh, but I needed to see if my brother was there.

He was there- alive. That's what I really wished, but...he wasn't even there- not dead and not alive.

"Paulo! Where are you?" I screamed, with tears streaming down my cheeks and onto my lips. I could taste the bitter saltiness rest on my lips, as I screamed my brother's name again and again, "Paulo! Paulo!"

I rested my head on the upside down seat and cried silently, as I hugged myself. "Please, please, come back." I leaned over to take a look again hoping, hoping that I was wrong. But nothing, absolutely nothing.

"Where did you go?" I screamed into the air. Then, the car all of a sudden fell on its roof, with me falling with it. Glass was all over me again. I brushed the glass off my body, seeing many cuts everywhere. "Help, help me! Someone... please... anyone..." again the tears, a waterfall cascade. I felt so afraid. "Please, God. Please don't let me die here," I mumbled out.

I lay there just staring up at the floor, as my tears finally stopped rolling. I calmed myself down. *Okay, Lupita. Just don't think about it right now. Make a plan, yeah a plan will be good. He's probably...he probably went to get help.*

My thoughts started to race, thinking of places he could have gone.

The hospital or the police station...the firefighters? My breathing was finally steady, and as my adrenaline was slowing down, I could feel the sharp piercing pain of the glass digging into my back. Some pieces pierced my skin, drawing blood. Also, there were small trickles of blood on my palms.

Everything hurts, I thought. *Everywhere it hurts.* Then suddenly, I heard the slip of a shoe. Looking out the window from where I lay, I saw feet running across the car. I was just about to start thinking help was not coming... *Wait! Where was she running?* I scowled.

The woman had pink shoes with blood droplets splattered on them, making it look like dark tiny roses. Then, I noticed the brown dusty sky from out the window, as it started to settle down, blanketing everything and everyone.

I was straining my eyes, trying to see through the thick dust and starting to crawl out the broken window but stopped. Then, I heard it: the terrified and agonizing screams and moans everywhere. My eyes formed huge saucers. I gulped and felt fear crawl through my skin.

"Agh!" I could hear a woman screaming and screaming. It wasn't like in the movies. The scream was real. The scream could make your bones shiver, as the blood-curdling scream pierced you like a knife.

I started to feel out of breath, as the screams and moans echoed all around me. My eyes darted everywhere, looking at the dusty curtain fall from the sky.

I can't take this! I screamed in my head, as I began struggling to get out again. I rolled over and felt the glass slide off me. Thousands of sharp pieces where everywhere below me, as I inched myself out the broken window, finally pulling myself out of the car and onto my feet. I turned around and around, dancing in circles as I saw the devastation.

Brushing myself off again, I looked down at my bloody palm when I felt slight pain. Small cuts were everywhere along my hands. I crouched down and reached back into the car, grabbing my bag. I pulled out the school's athletic uniform and tried to rip it into pieces to tie around my hands, but I couldn't.

Movies are all lying. I remembered that always worked in movies. I instead reached back into my bag and pulled out my scissors. It took some effort and patience, but I finally was able to cut pieces and tie them around my palms. Keeping my mind on that one task helped me better tune out what was around me. That is until I was done bandaging my hands. Then, my mind focused again to... well, everything.

No wonder no one is helping anyone...everyone is hurt or...dead. My eyes lingered upwards to a man atop rubble. His face looked away, but his arm was pointing down at me, as small drops of blood fell onto the littered street in front of me.

I looked away, dropping the scissors with a clatter and hugged my body. I was struggling to see as I made my way across the street. There were many people on the ground not moving, and the ones that were screamed and moaned. Some were so twisted and turned into odd angles that they couldn't move at all.

"Help me, please." Everywhere there were these types of pleas, and I couldn't just stand there and do nothing, so I ran over to someone in an upturned car and helped an older man from the passenger seat.

"Please," he begged. "My son... is he okay?" I looked over, and the only other person was the driver and his eyes were open and lifeless. "I'm sorry," shaking my head. I started trying to unbuckle him when his arms just suddenly dropped down. I knew what that meant. I had to check his pulse, and as I figured, nothing was there.

Gulping and crying silently, I moved away when another scream came from behind me. A woman, with her back on fire, came running from a smoking café. Her hands were flapping back and forth, trying to swat it out. Without thinking, I ran close to her and saw a man in a suit lying face down. I quickly pried his jacket off and ran over to the woman.

"Ma'am, over here!" I screamed at her, while holding the jacket up in front of me. She was then on fire everywhere. I kept trying to get her, but my own fear slowed me down, as I tried to stay away from the flames. All of a sudden, the building right beside me exploded, and both the woman and I fell down. My ears were ringing a little bit. I groggily got up, but the woman from the fire didn't. She no longer screamed, and I didn't know what to do. Making up my mind in a split second, I started to beat out the fire until I was able to put it out.

"Miss," I whispered to her. I could see her chest faintly moving up and down ever so slowly. I couldn't do anything, and I didn't want to keep seeing her, but I stayed there. A few seconds later with me just standing there, I saw her body give out its last breath. I cried and walked...no, I stumbled away. *If I try to help, everyone is just going to end up dying. I have to focus. I can't try helping. I just can't. I'm afraid if I don't think of something else, I just might stop entirely and be nonexistent. This is all too scary. I can't do this.* My mind flashed these thoughts, but I knew I had to be strong. Strong for my brother.

My brother is alive. I'm sure of it, I thought. "But, where are you, Paulo?" I looked at the feet of a body, and I urged myself to look at the face, to see if it was my brother... but I just couldn't. *My brother is alive. He's just... he's getting help. And the best place to get help is...* I looked around again, scanning as far as I could see. I saw someone leaning over a person on the ground... *He's at the hospital. Yes, that's it. He's at the hospital.*

Someone ran brushing against me, and I saw many more people run by me. They started to come from every direction. Sometimes, when they were running from the opposite direction toward me, I would see their eyes. They were big and wide. Every single one of them had eyes wide with fear and confusion. That's how I probably looked to them, too. Although the only difference was I was just standing there too much in fear to move.

"Help me!" A little girl went running to people, asking for help but many just kept running by. I could see a few people linger back, looking at her, and a couple with their own crying baby in their arms asked the girl to come with them urging her. "No, please! It's my mom; she's not breathing," she begged them.

"Where is she?" I asked urgently. "I'll help." The couple just left, and the people lingering turned around and kept running, too.

The little girl stared up at me in disbelief. "You...you'll help?"

"Yes, I will. I promise. I will. Now hurry! Let's go!" I reached for her hands, and she grabbed mine quickly, tugging me forward. Her hands were covered in dirt, and some of her knuckles were bleeding, but I just followed her into the dust. The little girl tugged me along across the street and over to a car that was directly in front of an alley, which we entered.

"Come on. Come on. Hurry," she urgently said, as I made my way over to the car. Once we were inside the alley, I looked up to see the tangle of ladders and walkways on the verge of collapsing, and pieces of bricks and plaster came tumbling down every so often.

"Hurry!" she yelled, turning around to me.

"Okay, okay." I hurried after her, finally on the other side of the alley, but I couldn't see where she went.

"Hey, where..." I started to say, looking for her when she appeared, popping up from behind a car.

"She's over here. Please, hurry." Tears started to fall down from her face, leaving clear streaks as her face was covered in dirt.

I quickly went over and saw her kneeling down beside a woman. "Okay, okay," I said to myself. "Step back, please." I gestured to the little girl, and she moved back, just right behind me, silently crying and biting her thumbnail.

Think! Think! I thought to myself, as I tried to remember how to do CPR. I nervously looked down at her face and checked for a pulse.

"Okay, she has a faint pulse, I think, but she has a pulse. That's good. Next, listen to see if she's breathing," I started to say.

"She's not breathing! I checked! Please hurry! I don't want her to die. Please, please, please!" the girl cried more tears.

"Right, right. Okay then. Not breathing. Tilt head back..."

"Please, just do it! Don't say, just do it! Hurry and do it!" The girl screamed into my ears.

I placed my hands over her mom's chest right in the center, my fingers intertwined and my elbows locked. With the palms of my hands, I began to press down and up and down, again and again. "One and two and three and four," I quickly started to count.

"Mom," the girl screamed. "Mom, please wake up! Mom!"

After I reached around thirty, I tilted her head back and began mouth-to-mouth resuscitation. There was nothing, no movement. The little girl looked at me then back to her mom on the floor, and the girl covered her face.

"One and two and three and…" I kept going, as I heard the girl move away from me and over to some rubble, making a clattering noise. I tilted her mom's head back again and blew as much air into her as possible. Two short breaths, lasting about two seconds, and I leaned and listened again. There was no movement of her chest or breath coming out, so I began again. I was not going to give up. I was not going to let the little girl be motherless.

"One and two and three and…" The woman immediately drew in air and started coughing and gasping for more air. I leaned back to smile at the little girl, but she was digging threw a big mound of rubble, and I saw her start to dig out a person under there.

"Ma'am, you'll be okay." I rubbed the woman's back, as I leaned her to her side. "Stay calm and breathe. I'll be right back." I ran over to the little girl, and she looked over at her mom and then at me smiling, and we started to dig.

"Dad!" the girl screamed happily, as we finally dug out her father. His back was to us, and he started to move, getting up, and the mother rushed to my side, helping him stand. In his arms, he held a crying baby. All of them were covered in dirt and dust, and the father was crying, as they hugged each other.

I moved back to let them have their moment to rejoice that they were still alive- all of them together. I smiled and cried; then, my smile faltered, and I cried again, but not for happiness, but for the pain and sudden lowliness. The thought that I might not have anyone made my heart break. If he's not alive, if my brother is dead out there, I would be the only one left here.

I am the only one left my mind briefly flashed that thought.

Then, there was a very loud rumble, as a whole building came down somewhere down the street. Glass shattered and concrete slabs came down from above, crashing to the ground. Deeper and more terrified screams came from there, followed by their bodies, as they swarmed all around us. There was no choice but to go with the crowd or else be stampeded down. I saw the little girl and her mother, but then, I lost track of them. I suddenly felt a large push, not like the one that flipped the car but still a stronger push of air, followed by specks of concrete, glass, dust, and dirt.

I ran and ran with the crowd, until there was finally enough room to go by the sidewalk or anywhere there was shelter. *I'm never going to see that family,* I thought, *or know if they made it out from the stampede of people.*

I suddenly realized that I was alone when I heard nothing. No screams, no moans. I was completely alone, except I could feel something watching me, something staring at me from the street where I had just come. I tried to peer through the dust, and I made out a large bulky dark figure. I could sense the coldness from it, just like you can feel the heat from the sun shining down on you. This...thing was radiating coldness and...and fear.

This thing isn't human. Just then, a small light flew overhead, and when I looked back at where the figure was standing, it was gone.

A deep terrifying scream came from the sidewalk I was on from back down the street. The scream was different. I could feel the pain and agony, and that's when I heard a dragging noise. I stopped where I was. Fear was forcing me to that spot as I just listened.

Something is wrong. Something is very, very wrong right here. A thousand thoughts ran through my mind, but not one came into focus. I just couldn't bear for my thoughts to be right.

Through the dust, I saw a woman with one leg and fresh blood gushing out everywhere, as she crawled on her arms towards me.

My eyes widened even more to the point where I could feel the tiny dust particles strike my eyes. I could feel my entire body tremble, as she came closer and closer. The woman had long blond hair with dark splatters of blood at the tips and black soot covering a few strands along the top. She had a beautiful face, but her right eye was half shut, and there was a waterfall of blood coming out. There was a deep cut on her left cheek with fresh blood running down onto her neck. She had a black and white checkered blouse with what were probably black pants, but then my attention was driven to her legs. One of them was severed at her knee with veins, muscle and a lot more blood trailing behind it. The other was twisted at the knee with the pants ripped, showing the bluish leg with a sandal on the foot.

I quickly looked back at her face to try to stop the urging temptation to throw up and faint. Though when I looked, I saw her good eye. It did not show fear or register pain in it. Instead, her dark bloodshot eye had more of a determined look in it, as if she was not going to stop. She was not going to give up no matter what- until she reached her destination.

She kept crawling until she was passed me. And, I didn't turn around. I dared not too. I couldn't see her go. Fear still rooted me to the spot, and I was just staring at the bloody trail she was leaving behind. The thought *I hate blood*, passed through my mind briefly as I kept staring at it.

Then, I felt my stomach lurch as I vomited in my mouth. I don't know if I swallowed it back down or just let it drivel down my mouth, but I felt my eyes roll to the back of my head and everything went dark as I fell backwards onto the hard asphalt street.

The Journey is Just the Beginning

I ran.

I found myself in front of a fiery wall of cars, right in front of the street smoke, billowing in every direction. I saw the fire engulfing the buildings left and right, but quickly turning, I saw a small entryway to the right. The front building was already in flames and an iron gate was tangled open, so I ran through the gates.

"Help me!" A man yelled from a second story balcony that had smoke pouring out from a half-open sliding door.

I found myself in an apartment courtyard with palm trees broken in half and uprooted, windows broken outwards and inwards, umbrellas, chairs, and tables all over the area. There were people wandering around streaming out bloody, confused, and in a daze. Dogs and cats were running around the courtyard, crazily barking or cowering.

"Let's go! Come on, Nicky," a man grabbed his daughter's hand as she looked up, her hands running through her hair as she started to tremble.

"Dad, where's Penny?" Nicky yelled, as her father pulled her out through an archway, leading out of the courtyard as other people ran through.

I quickly ducked as an explosion came from one of the higher buildings, bursting outward, and then, there was a cracking noise. The sudden cracks and pops made me look up as the balconies from that side of the building started to crumble away. I quickly jumped out of the way, as it came down near where I was standing.

Covering my head, I hid behind a bush, as fiery debris rained down and littered the ground. Opening my eyes, I saw a cat right in front of me, hiding and hissing at me. A small nametag that had a dog's bone hung from its neck. It read *Penny.*

Penny rushed at me, scratching my cheek and jumping from my back. She ran and ran. Taking her que, I jumped up as well. The courtyard was completely abandoned, no people, no animals, just fire starting to spring up in every direction.

I turned and headed where Nicky and her dad went. I ran through a dark short hallway, with sudden cracks appearing along the grey concrete floor. Panicking, I ran faster and faster. The ceiling and even the floor gave way and fell downwards, along with the walls. I almost made it out, when from the corner of my eye, I saw a stairway leading upwards into the building and a woman with a bright neon pink shirt hugging herself sitting on the stairs. My feet carried me away out the doorway, as I passed her and as the building came down behind me.

Still running, I felt my feet get tangled and I tripped, as I became engulfed by the dirt and dust of the building. Then, a hard but soft object fell down from the sky. The air escaped my lungs as I fought to get it back.

"One. Two. Three. Four," I counted. "Five. Six." Air returned to my lungs slowly. I stayed there in that safe cocoon for a few minutes, just closing my eyes and breathing, focusing on that.

Looking up, I saw a purple couch with flower decorations. I struggled to move it, but it wouldn't budge, so I wiggled from under it, through a small opening to the rubble underneath me.

"Hey, give me your hand, kid," a man in a baggy tee shirt completely covered in dust said from behind me. "Come on, kid," he beckoned his hand in front of me.

"Devon! Hey, man. I found someone down over here," another man yelled, as I gave Devon my hand and he helped me up.

"Hey, kid. What's your name?"

"Johnny. My name is Johnny." I gulped, looking around me as the entire apartment I just came from was all over me, well under me or on the ground level. A few wooden beams and walls were still standing. "What happened?"

"I think the ground gave way. Like one of those sinkholes I think."

"Devon, man! Come on. I can hear crying down here!"

"Alright, Johnny. There are some people helping each other just down the street and to the right." Devon pointed the directions to me, as he turned and ran to help the other man.

I started moving when I almost tripped. I didn't bother looking. I just kept moving with my eyes watery, as I kept my eyes straight ahead.

That woman didn't make it, I thought. *That woman didn't make it, and I almost didn't make it.* I stopped, and my head went up. My eyes saw the sun barely penetrating the dark brown dust. A coughing fit suddenly hit me, making me double over.

Then, a quick flash. I remember myself coughing like that. I remember coughing and blood coming out of my mouth, as my hand held pieces of glass. I remember seeing in front of me a glass plane broken and biting cold water swallowing my feet. *That's weird.* I don't remember any of that ever happening to me.

"Help, please!" a man's hand shot up from the ground grabbing my ankle. Startled, I yelped and jumped back. "No, wait! Please, help me," he begged.

Crouching down, I peered down, and the guy was buried between two slabs of a wall. "I'll go get help, okay."

"No, wait. Please, don't leave me." The guy sounded tired.

"I'm going to get you some help. Don't worry, okay," I assured him, as I got up looking for Devon and his friend.

"Please," he slid his hand back down the opening, and he lowered himself to where I couldn't see him.

"Wait, come back! Come back!" I crouched down again, laying and peering again between the slabs.

"I'm just so tired," he said from the darkness.

"I'll try to find a way to get you out, okay?" I asked him, waiting for a reply as I lay there trying to see him. "Hey!"

Quietly, he said, "I'm still here."

"I'll get you out, okay? Just hold on, okay." I still lay there waiting for his response. *Come on, Johnny. Come on, man! Come on!* I argued with myself in my mind. *Get up and look for a way to help,* but I still lay there waiting for his response. *Oh, no. I think he's gone now.* I jumped to my feet, starting to remove all the trash around the slabs.

"What..." I heard him weakly say.

"I'll get you..." Just then, a sudden blood-curdling cry made me scramble from the ground and move back a few steps. I heard what sounded like the man being torn apart.

I panicked and ran and ran. Running away from that area, my arms pumped back and forth. My breathing was jagged and in short bursts. Finally, down the street I stopped. Short of breath and eyes wide, I had my hands on my knees. My body was sweaty and flushed. I felt myself heating up, and my mind became dizzy.

"W-what was that?" I asked myself; my own voice sounded strained as if it weren't mine at all.

"Dad!" A scream echoed out across the street, along with the roars of fires and alarms. It also pierced through my head as another sudden flashback came to me.

My mind went back to the letter on my desktop. The letter I wrote to my father.

Dear Dad,

I'm sorry. This is probably the hundredth time I've written this, but I need to get this perfect. I never knew you but you know that. Or, I hope you do. But what does that matter anyway? I never knew you, and you never knew me, and that makes me so angry.

The windows of a car exploded outward followed by the horrible smell of hair burning. *My dad,* I thought. "I have to find my dad," I said to the dust. *He's my father. He's all I have left. But why did I write that letter... I knew my dad. I...* In the back of my mind, strange thoughts were bouncing back and forth: a car accident, a funeral, drowning, a party, but I couldn't focus on one thought exactly.

"I have to find him." *I don't know what any of this means, but I have to.* I rounded the corner, going to my right. I headed that way. Devon said there would be help *and* I'll ask if they know where the university labs are. Everything is going to get so much... better.

Ahead of me was a group of people with their backs to me, shuffling slowly forward. Moaning and crying, some people were being carried in makeshift stretchers or on other's backs. All covered in dust, they looked so...so lifeless.

"The journey is just beginning, kid," an old man shuffled, looking at the ground and holding his forearm with a dry blood cased rag wrapped around it.

"Yeah," I raised an eyebrow to his back. "The journey is just beginning." I began following the crowd. I guessed everyone was going in the same direction.

"Please keep moving forward," a police officer on top of her cruiser repeated, as other people went up to her asking questions.

"Have you seen this woman here?" a couple said, holding up a picture. "She's my mom, and she was with us when..."

"Please, my kids are at the..."

"What's going on here?"

"Please, my mother!"

"The school! Where's the school?"

"Have we been bombed?"

I stood around the crowd below the cruiser. "Where is the university?" My question was only drowned out by everyone else's questions.

"Please..." the officer looked straight ahead; her voice was shaky. "Just keep..." Gulping a sob, she continued loudly, "Just please keep moving forward. We have medical responders and food and water."

As the crowd dispersed, a new one took its place, but everyone else seemed to lose faith when the officer couldn't help them. Some people still stood around or behind the officer, repeatedly asking their questions and getting mad and forming a bigger crowd.

"Sir," I asked a man dressed in an apron around his waist. "Do you know where the university is?"

Shaking his head, he said, "Sorry, kid. I don't know where that's at."

As I continued down the street, more people started to seep from alleys and other streets onto the main one. We all had to start moving from the sidewalk to the street to the other side of the sidewalk and through a whole lot more twists and turns, as cars and crumbled buildings stood in our path. Almost every storefront had its windows broken along the way, but instead of looters taking things, there seemed to be a line of people running back and forth carrying food, clothing, mattresses, water and blankets.

In front of me, two men suddenly came out of a store. Its windows were completely smashed. They ran out so fast, half the things they brought out fell over.

"Hey wait," I reached down to pick up a few small palm-size boxes. "You dropped your... needles?" I asked, seeing as the boxes in my hand and on the floor were all sewing needles.

"Thanks, kid." One of the guys came back, snatched it from my hand and kept running not bothering to pick up the ones on the floor.

Finally, after a while of walking, I came into the center of a roundabout, where there were hundreds of people. All around me, there were people hurt or still in a state of shock. An ambulance parked on the side of the road had set up a makeshift emergency room, with the paramedics and a few other people running back and forth to injured victims, either stitching them up or holding down on them, as blood seeped out of wounds.

"Please, if you are not hurt, move to the café to my left!" A man yelled atop a busted Hummer. "If you are injured move forward to the parking lot of the hotel to my right!"

"Is there any place where my baby is at?" A woman shouted, her red teary eyes looked the same as many of the people all around me.

"Ma'am, further information will be in the fountain area just up ahead," a woman beside the Hummer came and told her.

"Again," she shouted, "there is further information straight ahead. Just please stay calm. We are all here to help!"

Everyone was already splitting up, as the man and woman kept repeating their words, and the people all around still looked as though they were confused.

I followed the crowd splitting off to the fountain. *Find my dad,* I thought. *Just find my dad, and I won't worry about anything else.*

All the vehicles were pushed out of the way except for a bus, which was being worked on. Its front hood and back hood were both open. Around the fountain, which was cracked and broken on one side, all the water pooled to the sides into the drainage. There were a few people in dusty suits, taking down names or talking to the people. I waited in a line that seemed to snake all over the place.

"Excuse me, sir," I asked a man in a dusty black business suit with black trimmed glasses, as soon as it was my turn. "I need to know how to get to the university from here."

"Kid," he looked down at me. "I think it's best to stay here until help arrives."

"Please, sir," I begged. "I need to find my dad."

"What's your name?"

"That doesn't matter. Can you please tell me how to get to the university?"

Suddenly, a woman appeared from the park besides the ambulance screaming, "IT'S THE END!" She was scratched in the arms and bleeding from cuts around her neck and shoulders. She went up to the people around her. "IT'S THE END OF ALL TIMES. THERE IS NO ESCAPE. WE ARE ALL..."

"Shut up!" A woman ran over and immediately slapped her. Several people also ran over. Some grabbed the second woman, and some were yelling at the screaming woman.

"This is not God's will!"

"This is a damn terrorist attack. I tell ya!"

"I DON'T BELIEVE IN GOD, YOU STUPID PEOPLE! ALL OF YOU LISTEN," she screamed, drowning out the people. "I'VE BEEN TO THE EDGE, AND IT JUST STOPS. IT JUST STOPS," she yelled out hysterically.

"What the hell do you mean?" the man yelling it was a terrorist attack yelled back. "We all know it was damn terrorists!"

"George," a man came up grabbing his shoulder. "Ignore the lunatic."

All around me, people stopped to listen, to whisper to their neighbors, most not paying attention and still talking to the helpers around the fountain, while others were yelling at her, screaming obscenities.

The woman went over to George and grabbed him by the shirt, staring up at him. She hissed out, "I've been to the edge of the city, and there's nothing."

"Get off of me you freak!" George pushed her away.

She fell to the floor, hugging her body, rocking back and forth whispering, "There is no escape. You understand- no escape. We're stuck here. No escape. No escape."

"Come on, sweetie." An older woman walked over and draped a bath towel over her. "I'll take you to get some help."

The people around the fountain started back flipping through papers and talking to the long lines and crowds of people.

"Sorry about that, kid." He shook his head. "That's not the first time it's happened. We already had at least ten people scream that. Poor guys. They've all lost it, probably from what they saw out here."

"Please, sir. I need to find my dad," I said impatiently.

"My name is James." He held out his hand to me.

I didn't shake it.

"Listen, kid. We could use some extra help around here."

"Are you going to help or..."

He cut me off as he scowled. "It's not safe out there all right, kid! If you go, you'll just get hurt, okay. Help will arrive here soon, and your dad is probably..." he trailed off as I felt myself get shivers.

"He's not...he's not dead," I said angrily, making my hands into fists.

"Listen, kid. Please, just listen." He raised his hands up. "We really need help around here. I'm sorry, but I can't have you going out there."

"You can't stop me," I looked at him, refusing to show myself crying.

"I can't stop you, no. But, you can help out and rest a little," he sighed running his hand through his hair. "Whatever." He shook his head, seeing as he wasn't making any progress with me. "The university is just a few miles north. Just cut across the park diagonally." Pointing with his finger, he quickly went back to work.

Suddenly, gunshots rang out, and I ducked down, along with everyone around me.

"Kid!" James crawled down beside me. "Come on! Get behind the fountain!"

I crawled, along with the other people James urged behind the fountain. People screamed and crouched or burst out every now and then into tears. I saw three people with guns drawn fill a bag from the makeshift emergency floor, with bottles of pills and others with food and water.

"Kid, get down!" James pushed my head down, as I lost sight of the robbery.

"Please, no!" Someone shouted, "My brother... he needs them... he's..." A gunshot rang out followed by a woman screaming in pain and other people screaming, too.

"Please, just stop it! We can all help each other," the man from the Hummer yelled out.

I don't know what happened, but I heard a shuffle followed by someone else shouting, "Get them!"

James held me down by the shoulder, as he peered out.

"What's going on, James?"

"A group of people got one of the gunman. They..." He didn't finish the rest, as suddenly again gunshots rang out. "The police woman's shooting at them now."

I cringed as every gunshot rang out. Each shot echoed, and the people around us screamed out, mixing in with the woman still screaming and crying.

I don't want to die, I thought. *I want my dad. I want to know if he's okay.* I held my eyes shut. As I lay there, the gunshots still rained through the air. The people were screaming and crying, and my body was trembling.

Please. Please. Please, I'll do anything. Just please, don't let me die. I opened my eyes just as a gunshot rang right above us, and as James ducked his head down, pieces of the fountain fell down on us. Agh! I covered my eyes with my hands, quickly rubbing them. I was blinded as sharp pain stung my eyes, and my ears rang as the people around me screamed in terror.

"Kid, stop! Let me help," James hissed as the firing stopped abruptly.

"Enough please. Just stop it," a woman's voice rang out.

"There are pieces in my eyes," I said to James.

"I know, kid," he whispered. "Just keep them shut for bit. I think it's over now."

Just as he said that, the officer's voice rang out, "Everyone, please! It's over now." Several people started to clap at her. "People, please," she hushed the crowd. "I want you to do what you can to help the people around you. We are all in this together, and we will stick together as the community we are!"

"Come on." I felt James' hand grab onto my forearm, as he helped me to my feet. "I'll help you clear your eyes."

As I blindly followed James, I could hear the woman's crying getting closer and closer. *Don't let me trip, please. I don't want any more pain,* my lips mouthed my thoughts.

"You say something, kid?"

"No... James, all I have to do is pour some water in my eyes and let the pieces get watered out," I said behind him.

"I know," he groaned sharply in pain.

"Are you okay?" I asked. Then, I almost tripped as he caught me.

"I'm good, kid. Watch your step. There's some rubble." He led me up the sidewalk. "Alright we're here."

"Put these things back and continue your rounds," a woman's stern voice said right in front of us.

"Yes, Dr. Pen," someone replied leaving.

"Hey, excuse me," James called out.

"Not right now. Report your injuries to one of my staff. I need to stop that woman's wailing," replied the doctor.

"Wait, please," James pleaded followed by a low grunt only I could hear.

"Ma'am, I am just going to cover up your wound. The bullet just grazed you." The doctor tried calmly to stop the woman.

"Is my brother okay though?" the wailing woman said between sobs.

"Hey, you. Please, help us," James said out loud.

"Sir, I need you to wait over there," said a man's voice in front of us.

"I told you, ma'am. Your brother...your brother did not make it. We're moving him out already. We need to make room for more people," the doctor said slowly.

"I know. I know," she said between sobs. "But, is he okay? You're going to help him right, doctor?"

"Yes, ma'am," the doctor said flatly. "Now lie down. David!" she called out. "Patch this woman up."

"Sorry, sir. I have to..." I felt James's hand slowly let go, but that time when he did finally let go, I heard him fall down.

"James!" I yelled out, as I reached down for him. I blearily tried opening my eyes, and with them watery and blurry, I could make out James on the floor.

"I got you, sir. I got you!" The man in front of us said, as he helped James get up.

"Agh!" James yelled out, as the man let go slowly, setting him down on the floor and revealing James' suit front soaked in blood.

"Doctor!"

"Help him!" I yelled. "Help him!"

"David, what's...!" The doctor came running and as soon as she saw us, she sprinted faster and crouched beside James.

He winced in pain, as the doctor led him to a mattress. I started to follow when David held me back by the arm.

"Sorry, kid. I'm going to have to ask you to wait at the café, and I'll have someone fetch you over."

"Wait, I just...uh. I need to wash my eyes out. The gunshots broke pieces of the fountain, and I have little pieces of them in my eyes." I know my eyes were completely watery and red and the rapid blinking only helped with my pleading more.

"Okay, come on. I'll help." David walked me to the opened back of the ambulance where he washed my eyes out. "Okay, tilt your head back and open your eyes wide."

"Thank you." I wiped the water off my face with the sleeve of my shirt.

"No problem, dude. Martha!" he yelled as a girl in pink dyed hair came around the ambulance with a clipboard. "Take his name and tell him to wait at the café," David said behind his back, as he went into the rolls of mattresses and blankets on the floor.

"Hi, my name is Martha." Looking down at her clipboard, she uncapped a sharpie as she pressed down on the paper. "May I have your name?"

"Johnny. Can I go see James now?"

"James is the one you're here for? Does he have a last name, and what is his relation to you??

"I don't know his last name, and he's just a friend."

"Okay, when James is better, I'll come and find you." She walked away leaving me alone. Well, as alone as you can be when you're surrounded by hundreds of people. I sat at the end of the bumper and ran my hands through my hair, brushing little pieces of the concrete and plaster out.

It's my fault, I sighed, with the palms of my hand resting on my temple. *If I just would have not been there. If I would have just...* agh! Suddenly, I heard a small scream to my left. No one else had heard it, as I looked around. *I have to help* ran through my head. I got up quickly and took a few steps around the ambulance when the scream came again. *It sounds far away. I have to hurry...or I should get help.* I staggered on the heels of my shoes.

The scream continued but slowly died out while I just stood there. *Whoever it was probably was dead by then. I can't help anyway.* I justified myself, but I started walking to where the scream had come from. My feet kept carrying me, as I passed two big cars, blocking the street, except for a small entryway big enough for four people- shoulder to shoulder.

As soon as I stepped across the cars, I tensed up and froze. In front of me, covering every inch of the street, were bodies. Some were covered in blankets, a few in body bags, and the rest with a piece of clothing covering their face. Stacked feet to head with a few walkways between each roll, there were bodies upon bodies upon bodies. Straight in front of me, a woman in a bright red jacket was in a fetal position.

Gulping, I moved forward very slowly. My eyes trained on the red jacket, I breathed out and in the whole way while walking, trying to keep my thoughts from realizing I was in a cemetery. *Just the bodies weren't buried was all. Dammit, Johnny!* I was right on top of the woman. Her skin was ashy white. I crouched down to shake her.

"Miss?" Gulping, I could feel the air around me dip down, almost to a freezing point, and I could see my breath in front of me. *What's going on?* Suddenly rising to my feet, I saw movement behind a car.

What the hell is that? My mind panicked, and my breath quickened, as I looked through the dusty windows and saw something that couldn't be there. Something that shouldn't exist. Behind those windows was a creature with black eyes, a few sharp teeth in the front of its mouth, and no cheeks. I could see all of the rest of its teeth and curling and uncurling hair, with small skulls that hissed out their tongues, all looking at me as I looked back.

The blood pounded in my ears, and my heart raced to get away. The thing tilted its head, and with a very long tongue, licked up and down the window. The tongue extended from one end of the window to the other. Its head was still. I couldn't utter a word; my mouth remained shut, my teeth clattered together, and my nose exhaled and started to burn from the coldness.

It started to laugh, and I could feel its laughter in the very core of my body. It seemed to echo in my bones, as it raised an arm. Its claw-like hands scratched the window in front of it. Afterwards, there was a screeching sound, as it left its human-like naked body with peeling white skin and walked away.

"Hey, kid. You're not supposed to be back here," a man yelled at me, along with another man carrying a body with them. They both gently put the body down, and one of the men started walking up to me. I looked around. Everything was all back to normal, well with the dust still in the air.

"Come on, kid," the man said. "I know you lost a loved one, but the doc said, 'Just to be safe, they have to...' Jesus! Darra!" The man crouched down to the woman with the red jacket, but once he touched her jacket, the body disintegrated and flew upwards...turning to dust. "Jesus! Jesus!" he yelled out, stumbling backwards.

"What's going on?" The other man came running by and looked from me to his friend to the clothes on the floors. The first man wide eyed jumped up and stumbled, landing on one knee and ran between the cars. "I don't know what happened, kid, but you can't be here." He reached for my arm, gripping it, but I wormed out.

"Fine!"

"Fine. Pay your respects to whomever you're here for," he sighed and walked away.

What was that thing and why did this woman just disappear? No, not disappear. Why did she turn to dust? And why hasn't the dust settled already? I quickly ran to where the creature was behind the car. The entire side of the car had five deep holes in it, forming five jagged long lines until the end near the taillight. On the window though, it had written three words. Three words that made my skin crawl. Three words that made me rethink and question all that was happening.

NOT YOUR TURN.

On the window, it had scratched those three words meant for me. I slowly walked back between the cars. My mind was unable to process anything, but my feet carried me around the ambulance, across the fountain with bullet holes on the top and middle of it, and into the park.

I felt myself disappear into the dust...*the dust that belongs to the people. No...the dust that is the people.*

****

I woke up with my head pounding and hurting in my back. I rubbed my head, and it felt sticky. I pulled my hands back, and they were covered in blood. My eyes immediately closed shut, as they rolled back.

I fainted again, I said to myself as I finally came to. There was no longer any pain or pounding, but I did feel a bit dizzy as I got to my feet. I looked around and groaned, as I dreamed of being home in my bed, surrounded by the softest pillows I could imagine. I felt my stomach do flips, as I covered my mouth as quickly as possible and ran to a cab and vomited by the passenger seat. Wiping my mouth, I looked at the window and screamed. There in front of me was a dead man with his head resting against the window with blood splattered on it.

I can't stomach any of this. My mind started seeing those bodies as another part of my environment. *How can I be used to this already?* My stomach was still jumping up and down every time I saw a body, but not as much as before when I would run.

I started walking up through mounds of rubble with limbs sticking out, through streets with doorways or elevators from the buildings all around. The dust made everything look older, as if it had been there for a very long time.

Crying and screaming rang out, but it was just another part of the surrounding. *Why am I not showing emotion...why am I so indifferent towards this?* I wanted it to be a nightmare before, but now I've accepted it as it is.

"It hasn't even been a day." My voice sounded strange to my ears, well mixed in with cries, screaming, the roaring of fires, and the collapsing of buildings. Everything sounded strange. It was something to get used to, and I was getting used to it already.

The hospital! My mind screamed, almost forgetting the reason I was even out there. Looking around, I tried finding a sign that pointed to a hospital or a bus stop that had the maps on its boards. But through the thick dust, I had to walk along the sidewalks, or what space they had, to find something. Most of the street signs were gone, bent, or lying on top of the vehicles. After checking, none of the ones I found had any signs of a cross or hospital.

I started going down some stairs between two big buildings. There didn't seem to be much rubble there. There were even some trees still standing along the sides of those stairs, but I tripped on what felt like loose concrete. Luckily, I caught myself and kicked the piece down the rest of the stairs. Starting to walk down again and holding on to a rail that ran down the middle of the stairs, something at the back of my mind was screaming at me to stop.

I kept walking, choosing to ignore the warning. All around, the dust seemed to get thicker. *This is strange...why hasn't the dust settled already... Agh!* Screaming at the sudden surprise, my foot that was supposed to land on the next step or the floor just went right through. Almost falling down, I held onto the railing, as I shimmered my way up the jagged concrete stairs. Beneath me, pitch darkness spread out far below me and as far as I could see on the horizon.

Peering down, with one hand holding onto the rail and the other gripping the last step, I stared and stared for what felt like hours. My thighs burned, and my hands went numb, from holding too hard. I slowly made my way upstairs and once on top where I began, I fell to my knees, and tucking them in, I hugged my body.

"It's the end," I murmured. "It's the end..." I don't know how long I was there or how long I was rocking back and forth saying the same thing over and over, but looking up at the sky, still a thick hazy brown, I started wondering if time was even moving. Obviously, something was not right. Something had changed the physics of the normal world. It was a whole new world. There just can't be an endless drop. There can't be dust that doesn't settle. There can't be that bright light in the sky. My brother can't be gone.

Jumping to my feet, I sprinted up the steps, skipping two at a time. Rounding the corner, I ran. *That's all I had been doing lately.* I ran and ran, jumping over rubble piles of bricks and concrete all over the ground. I dared not look at any bodies and limbs I saw exposed. Climbing across cars and through a bus to get around, I noticed clothes and bags strewn everywhere and a few small mounds of dust. Going into an alley, I looked up. The metal railings jutted out between the old brick apartment.

I remember the first time I arrived to my brother's apartment. I asked him if I could go on the rooftop, and that was the first thing we did. With my luggage all in hand and my brother's as well, when he opened the door, I dropped everything. I had been so scared, felt so alone, and when I finally saw the city from his apartment, I was taken aback. Never in my life had I seen anything more beautiful. Sure, the air sucked and part of the view was blocked by another bigger building, but the sense that the entire concrete and glass valley was cased with people- all different types- wondering and living.

The lights coming on as the sun finally started setting was like the beginning of a song. When the music was picking up, the beats and rhythm were starting to flow, and the city was so full of it. Then, what felt like minutes seemed to be hours as my...mother. My head started to hurt as my memories started to change.

I...know, that can't be right. That never happened; it was my brother...wasn't it? My mother put her hand on my shoulder, and I turned around looking into her eyes. She was smiling, but her eyes were so sad, and I felt my eyes started to cry as well. I hugged her as she caressed my hair. "Shh shh ya estara bien mi nina," she comforted me, and I hugged her tightly.

That's not my memory...it's not. It was my brother. I looked around and kept walking forward. The alley was dark and brown. The end seemed to be blocked off, so I turned around. I started walking underneath the rails again and stopped right as I passed the ladder going up. Impulsively, I turned around and climbed on top of the first railing. I felt a creak and a snap, as I quickly fell against the rail, and one side of the metal rod sticking to the bricks pulled out.

Steadily, I started moving slowly, one inch at a time to the next railing, up the stairs. All the while, the creaks and groans made me hold my breath and remain silent. I was even afraid my own thoughts would disturb the rickety black metal walkways. Slowly, one step at a time, I went up and up and up, then finally on the rooftop. *Yes! But what possessed me to go up there?* My hands on my knees, I calmed myself down, seeing my surroundings as I looked up. *I think I came up here to remember.*

Yes, I have to remember him. I have to remember my brother. But, it was my mother who kept popping up in my head. Her beautiful black hair, her light green eyes with red around the outside of the irises, as if she had been crying. Her dark brown skin was smooth and perfect, as she held me in her arms. Her thin lips were smeared with red lipstick, matching her red and pink flower pattern blouse. She smelled like lavender, our favorite flowers, as she always put them in vases in the bathroom and the kitchen window. The view was always the wall of the opposite building, but she would put flowers on the window still and would pretend she was outside in a meadow.

That had been my favorite thing about her. She would smile at her own imagination, and every now and then, she would share it with me. She would say to close my eyes and picture this, "A beautiful pristine meadow with grass knee high, flowing with the wind and the rustle of leaves from the trees would finally reach you and it's blowing your hair everywhere." Of course, I would open my eyes, as I heard a whirling sound, and I'd see her holding a small fan in front of me, and we'd both laugh and smile.

I missed her very much. *But why can't I remember my brother in this city.* The rooftop should have brought back that memory, but it didn't. It felt as if... *It feels like my mind is lying to me.* Going back to the metal railings, I looked down and smiled.

I feel like a ninja. Deep down, I felt a little happy that my mind was pushing all the bad stuff away, though I don't know if that was a good thing or a bad thing. I turned around again and walked right to the edge, overlooking the city, and as I turned around, looking at the rooftop, I saw a sun chair with a pile of dust all over it. *Weird.* I ran my hand through it, letting it spill from my hands, then I wiped it on my pants. Looking out at the view, I saw just a wall of dust, barely making out the outline of the building across, for that matter any of the buildings surrounding me.

This city has no life.

Something slithered behind me. I tensed up, feeling suddenly cold. I turned around quickly when I felt a cold breath breathe down on me. Nothing. I wiped my head from left to right and still nothing.

"Hello," I whispered. *Lupita, come on. There is nothing in the dust.* "I've never said that before...and I've never talked to myself before."

The slithering sound came again, but that time I heard it from the railings. I ran over to them and peered down. Something long was moving down the railings, and with a thud, it landed to the ground. *That thing just dropped eight feet.* My eyes fell to the edge, and I saw a shiny goo like substance, a moldy green color snaking its way down.

I edged back. *I'm not sticking around here.* I ran looking for a door that would lead me through the building. Just when I was getting close, I saw a crow on top of another pile of dust with pants, shoes, and a shirt sticking out of the dust. Almost close... now passing the pile, the crow lifted its wings and instead of feathers, its bones were jutting out with black tar covering the body, and there was a dark patchy skull with claws on the ends of the wings. Screeching at me, I yelped and cringed, running to the silhouette of the door. The doorknob turned, but the door wouldn't budge. Pulling and pulling, I looked over my shoulder. There were then two birds staring at me with their black hollow eyes.

"Come on! Come on!"

Cree! Cree! Starting to flutter upwards, I looked at them while pulling the door. *That's impossible! They have no wings. They can't fly. They just can't.*

One of them flew at me, and I ducked just in time, as it hit the doorframe, leaving a small dent. It landed on top of me, and when it touched my skin, I felt it burn, a horrible searing burn that felt like my whole body was on fire. Pushing it away, I yanked the doorknob. It finally gave way, and I ran inside just as the other creature threw itself at the door, too.

Cringing, I crouched as those things started scratching at the door with their claws and screeching. Covering my head, afraid that at any moment they would break through, I started crawling down the flight of stairs. The echoes reverberated as I walked down the stairs, and I kept seeing piles of dust and clothes everywhere.

What is all of this? I asked myself as almost every step down had those mounds. Then, a scream sounded just as I passed the second floor door. Still crouching afraid that those things would break in and fly over me, I hesitated about getting out of there or going through the door. Without thinking, I pushed the door open, and no longer hearing the thuds, I stood up. The hallway was dark except for one window that showed the only light at the end of the hall.

"Hello?" I asked the empty space.

Clack, clack, clack, clack! Something darted quickly across the hall and into an opened doorway. My eyes strained to see, but I quietly hoped it was just a cat, as it moved swiftly. I slowly stepped into the hallway, going one step at a time. I soon passed the window, and to my astonishment, it wasn't broken. Almost everything else was, but I could barely see outside. I soon worked up my nerve to walk further, and from the last door to my right, there was a slight amount of light peering through a few windows, but otherwise, everything was in shadows. I hung at the open doorway and just gripped the frame.

I wanted to step inside and see if there was someone there, but my body didn't move and I dared not breathe. I wanted to believe. I so wanted to believe that everything would be okay, if I just stepped inside. So, that's what I finally did.

"Hello?" I whispered. "Hello is...is anyone there?" There was absolutely nothing. No sound, no "clack, clack" noise, just silence. But, it was a heavy silence. I could practically feel the air become heavy, and my body prepared for something lurking in the shadows.

I walked further into the apartment and peered into the nothingness. My nerves standing on edge, I was just ready to jump at any sudden movements. One step at a time. That's all I thought about.

"Okay, entering the kitchen," I slowly said, as I entered the kitchen and dining room. There was the slight smell of propane, but that might have just been my imagination, as I looked closely and noticed the stove was electric. *My nerves are really on edge.* My thoughts flashed, and I giggled to myself. *Nothing is going to come out and scare me. There is literally nothing in the shadows but shadows themselves.* Suddenly, in the living room, there was a large armchair that faced the wall, and it could hide someone.

"Bad idea! Bad idea!" I screamed to myself. "Do not, Lupita! Please, I beg you!" I walked slowly towards the chair; my breathing picked up radically. I literally begged myself, but my legs kept moving. My feet and I were right in front of the chair. Gulping, I silently tiptoed to the side of the armchair, and right there, sitting on the chair was a teddy bear. A sweet teddy bear that was the size of my arm and was very fluffy.

"Hey, little guy." I smiled and picked it up. "Who would leave you facing the corner? Have you been a bad boy?" I hugged the teddy bear and turned the chair around, making the scratching noise as it moved. I don't think I ever had a teddy bear growing up. It was more of a handmade doll passed down from generation to generation, but I had given it to my mother when she left, so she could remember me. I kind of wished I still had it with me. The teddy bear shall be a replacement for now.

I hugged it and squeezed it, smiling and then frowning, as I started getting lost in a memory that again shouldn't be there. I was sitting in the hospital waiting room, and I was staring at my mother. She was huddled in a corner. Her legs were up in the chair too, as she hugged that doll. Right across from me, I could see my teary red puffy eyes and a bandage across my forehead.

"Mom," I croaked, and she looked up at me. Quickly coming over to me, she sat beside me and held me. I had no tears left in me, but I knew she needed someone's shoulder to cry on.

"Ma'am," a nurse came over with a clipboard. "He doesn't have much time. We're not supposed to do this, but... come with me. I'll show you to his room. You can say your goodbyes before..." She left it at that. Both my mother and I jumped to our feet and followed her.

We followed her, but I felt myself slowing down. I could see my mother in front of me quickly getting away, not even bothering to look back. I knew who we were headed for. I knew it was not my fault, but still I felt responsible. I had distracted him, and then, the truck came and then, the broken glass. Then, the blood and the light in my eyes, with the voice behind it asking my name and to count to something.

I knew that if I kept going with them, I would have to say goodbye, but if I stayed there, just hiding in the corner somewhere, I wouldn't have to face it. I could pretend it never happened. I could... *I don't want to lose my brother.*

No, not these memories again. My head started throbbing again, but I forced myself to relax. *Too much is happening at once, and I just need to take it slowly.*

"Clack! Clack! Clack!" The sudden noise had me twisting my head quickly and looking everywhere, from the kitchen to the floor scanning my eyes in every direction.

I didn't know where to move, and I was terrified. I quickly sat on the chair behind me and picked my legs up. I started crying silently and hugged the teddy bear tightly. *Please. Please, make it go away. Just please make it go away.*

I closed my eyes and continued crying. After a while, I heard nothing, so I looked up and nothing. Nothing on the floor or ceiling, nothing in the corner, nothing anywhere but shadows, which my eyes had finally adjusted to, so I could fairly see more of everything.

I was about to step out and put my feet down, scared that something would grab my ankles, but thought better of it and slowly and steadily stood up on the chair and jumped. I didn't make it far, and I felt stupid. I should have paid attention as I landed. I slipped and landed face down before the noise began.

Clack! Clack! Clack! I turned around and sprinted out the door. Crashing against a tabletop and sending a vase crashing and breaking onto the floor. I kept running, and that's when I felt more. Then, I saw something that looked like a crab mixed with a cat fly right across. I quickly ducked down as it passed by, and I kept on running. Finally, as I reached the door, I slammed it shut behind me and leaned there, trying to catch my breath from that run. It felt as if I had run a marathon. Suddenly, the door behind me banged and shook as that clacking noise continued.

I screamed and held myself, hugging the teddy bear that was still in my hands. The door continued shaking, and I just couldn't take it anymore. I stumbled to my feet and sprinted down the hall, down the stairs, and out into the hazy world.

Run and Don't Die

In the park, I felt like I was walking through a desert. It was finally starting to get dark. I could faintly see the sun starting to move westwards, and curiously, I heard birds and insects. For some reason, I was afraid they wouldn't be there and it was going to be silent, but I would never take animals for granted again. My walk started there, and I thought I'd be alone, but they kept me company.

A duck started walking with me. *It probably wants some food.* I reached for my backpack looking for change, and I just grabbed air. *When did I lose my bag?*

"Sorry, little guy. I have no food." I stopped and looked at the little brown duck. It looked up at me and squawked; then, two more waddled up beside it. "Nope, guys. See no food." I emptied out my pockets and only pulled out some lint, which fell down. All the ducks looked at the piece of lint. I'll admit so did I, and when it hit the ground, the ducks looked back at me and squawked. I laughed at them, and they waddled away, but I kept laughing at their backs, and my stomach started hurting. I made my way to a bench and continued laughing hysterically and crying.

"Are you okay?" A woman's voice asked, as she appeared from the dust.

"Yes, sorry." I tried catching my breath, and I wiped my nose on the sleeve of my shirt. "Just some funny ducks is all." She looked at me in a funny way, and then, she smiled.

"I guess ducks can be funny," she giggled and just stood there. She was very pretty, well aside from a bruise on her cheek and small cuts, which I figured was from glass. I was getting good at naming wounds from where they came from.

"So, just taking a stroll through the park?" I don't know why but I didn't feel like myself. I knew I was putting up a front right then, so that I would be distracted.

"Yea, I just needed some air. I honestly thought the dust wouldn't be as thick here, but well..." She raised her palms upwards, "that's clearly not true."

I chuckled and looked around me. "The dust is of all the dead bodies, and I think we are in hell," I blurted out, as I dropped my smile and stared outwards.

"How old are you?" I was taken aback by her sudden words. She didn't acknowledge that I said that...*or did I even say it out aloud?* Her expression on her face was then sad and solemn.

"I'm sixteen. My birthday is next week." Actually my birthday was... my head started throbbing as memories quickly flashed by.

A park, my family, and my friends were grilling burgers and hotdogs and corn on the cob. Not my birthday but someone else's. "Happy birthday, Dad," I screamed, as I ran up to him, and he lifted me in his arms.

"There's my big boy," he tickled me, and I giggled and thrashed around in his arms.

"Put my boy down this instant or so help me," my mom sassed at him, with her hands on her hips.

"Mommy, help! He's gonna eat me alive," I pleaded giggling.

"Oh, no," she gasped her hands covering her mouth. "By the way, we will have to work on not using short words. Remember English is proper...well kind of." She winked at the both of us.

"Oh, boo," my father said. "Party pooper with your proper English." He smiled as he put me down.

"Awe, Mom. Why didn't you rescue me?" I asked, looking at her pouting my face.

"Oh, who said your dad was the monster?" She crouched down and started making goofy faces. "Run, or I'm going to eat you, my love and teach you proper English!"

"Agh, run! Dad, run." He gave the spatula to someone else, and we all went running around. And finally, they both grabbed me by my hands and lifted me up, swinging me back and forth.

I started crying as that memory flashed by. I wiped away the tears, but I couldn't talk. I was afraid I would somehow startle the memory away.

"Just keep remembering those happy memories," the woman said to me, as she smiled and walked away. I nodded my head, as she left into the dust.

I calmed myself down and got to my feet. *I am going to find my dad, and when I do...*a sudden scream came from the direction the woman had left in. I quickly sprinted towards where she had gone, but the path had split, and there were no more screams or any noise at all. No insects, no animals, and no people. Panicking, I looked left and right. *The sun was setting east, so I need to go north east, I think.*

I hope that woman was okay, but I was too scared to try to find her, so I ran away. *What was I going to do anyway? She's probably dust already.* I heard a crash from the water and felt a few droplets fall on my neck and the back of my hands. Doing a quick turn, I saw a slimy blue monster come racing towards me, and I don't even know if I had ever run faster in my entire life.

Screaming, I sprinted off the path, as it wound around to the right, and I quickly doubled my steps, as I went up a hill. I could feel the heavy breathing of the monster on my back, as it got closer and closer. Just as I got over the hill, a pile of clothes was right under me, and I jumped up only for the beast to swipe its huge claws at my feet. I felt myself flying a far distance, and I landed in a small pond. Quickly getting on my feet, I waded out. Completely soaked, I looked back and saw the monster more clearly. It was like a bull but with more than two horns on top of its head. I couldn't see any eyes, but it had outward horns, sort of like funnels sticking out. Its teeth were like needles, and they extended outwards and inwards, as it breathed in and out. It also had six thick legs, as it raced down to me.

"Help me!" I yelled, as I pulled myself out of the water. The only thing that answered my plea was some ducks that quickly ran into a bush. I heard a crash, as water flew upwards, and I again sprinted, with my shoes making a squishing noise, giving me away. Even if that thing was blind, I was going to die there.

I saw the path, starting to go up another hill. I was about to try to find another path when I heard a loud thud behind me, and the ground shook with it. I stumbled but righted myself and ran again up the hill. That time though, there seemed to be a large picnic area with lots of people.

"Agh," a woman screeching on a table alerted more people, as she pointed down at me. Several other people started screaming and shouting. I was getting closer and closer to them.

"Please! Please help!" I begged as I heard the first shot. Quickly, I fell to the ground face first and breathing hard. I covered my head with my hands and waited until I turned to dust. Instead, I heard more shots, and the monster come running faster and faster with its thuds and more screams and shouts. Finally, it stomped its way past me and roared up to the people.

"Oh, no." I looked up and saw the monster thrashing its head at the people. It was so chaotic, as everyone either started running, cowering, or beating the thing with sticks, bats, or shooting it. There was so much noise that what I started to fear I actually heard coming from the pond down below me. I looked over my shoulder and saw two of those big monsters starting to come up. The dust blocked my view, but one seemed smaller, and the other was much bigger.

I rolled out of the way and tried getting back up to my feet. Right when I did that, my shoes made another squishing sound, and I sprinted out of there. I didn't care if they heard or not. I didn't want to take any chances. I ran and ran and ran. Jumping over benches and going through a gazebo, I saw piles of clothes and dust being blown away. Blankets and old fashioned picnic baskets were strewn everywhere. I would jump right over them or go around them.

I reached a small building with a sign that showed a man, a woman, and someone in a wheelchair. I went through an open doorway, trying to catch my breath. *I think I'm ready to run a marathon.* I laughed at my own stupidity and quickly covered my mouth, afraid I was too loud. Looking both ways, I walking into the men's restroom and used a stall.

"Don't flush," someone in the next stall beside me suddenly said. I jumped up startled.

"I...I wasn't going to," I mumbled out.

He laughed suddenly. "Look at us having an awkward conversation in the bathroom during the end of the world." He chuckled, and I just raised my eyebrows.

"Yea, I guess so." I quickly finished my business and opened the stall to get out. "Are you coming out or are you staying there forever?"

He snickered at the closed door. "Probably stay here forever," he answered back casually.

"What! Why?" I shouted urgently.

He hissed at me quickly, "Keep your voice down, or we'll die right away." I ducked, afraid that those beasts would come crashing through the walls.

"You can come with me, and we can...I don't know... help each other," whispering, I felt like I was back at school, trying not to let the teacher overhear my conversations with my friends.

"No, I think I'll stay here."

I looked at the door with the most confused look on my face. "But why? There are monsters out there. I think it would be best to stay in a group to stick together."

"But, you're alone right now. So, I don't think you need me. I'll just get in the way."

"No, you won't. Trust me. Both of us together can make it. What's your name by the way?"

"My name is Alex, and no, I will stay put here. I mean you practically killed those people up in the picnic spot."

I was taken aback by the new information. "I...I didn't kill them." I stammered the last bit, trying to convince myself that I was right.

"Well, not outright, but you gave them a death sentence," he continued with sarcasm in his voice.

"Look, Alex. Are you going to come with me or not?" I was starting to get annoyed, and I was thinking of just leaving the guy behind.

"Like I said, no. Now, why don't you just go away?" That's when I noticed the squeak of the wheelchair, as I saw part of it from under the stall.

I can't just leave him here. He is going to die if I do. "Look, Alex. I promise I will..." I was cut off from his sudden outburst.

"Look, I don't need your sympathy!" He had raised his voice, but then lowered it, as he continued. "Just leave, okay. I'm sure you saw my wheelchair, and you know I won't make it out there so just...just leave, okay?"

Gulping, I lingered at his closed door, and after a while, I turned around and left. As I got close to the exit, I stayed still. *Just try one more time; just one more. If I can convince him and at least help him get out of this park. I can...I can what, Johnny?* I groaned in frustration, as I was having an internal conversation in my head... *Great! Now, I'm officially crazy. Oh well! This world is already crazy enough.*

I turned around and walked right back to Alex's closed door. "Look, Alex. I am not leaving here 'til you come out. I will get you help, but we need to get out of this bathroom and out of this park."

"You are one stubborn guy...What's your name by the way?" I think I could sense him smiling from behind the door.

"My name's Johnny, and you have my word, Alex." I moved my hand to the door handle and tried opening it and failed. "Come on, Alex. I said I'll help."

"Sorry, Johnny." I could hear the despair in his voice. "But, you better run...NOW!" He shouted the last part and continued shouting. "RUN, JOHNNY! RUN! GET OUT OF HERE!"

"Shh, stop. Stop, Alex. Stop! What are you doing?" I begged him to stop shouting.

"YOU BETTER GET OUT OF HERE, JOHNNY! THEY'LL BE HERE ANY SECOND!"

"Alex, come out!" I tried shaking the door again, but it was locked tight. I got on my knees and started to crawl down under, when he pushed me away.

"NOPE! JOHNNY, THIS IS FOR YOUR OWN GOOD! NOW, GET OUT OF HERE!" Just then the wall on the other side of the stall door was broken into, with pieces flying everywhere. And that's when the roar sounded, and Alex said his last words to me, before screaming for his life.

"RUN, AND DON'T DIE!"

"You idiot!" I banged my hands against the door frame, turned and ran out.

With my shoes making noises, I didn't want to stick around that park. So, I ran without stopping, tears slowly running down my cheeks. *I've gotten used to tears now, and I will now only shed them for the people I care about.* I spotted an exit out of that place and sprinted my last few paces there.

Just like almost every time I had stopped, I grabbed my knees and gasped for air. *Don't think about him. Just don't think about him.* My heart kept trying to feel sympathy, but I had to get myself together.

"Dad, please be alive. Please, let him be alive." I asked the dust all around me. It seemed it had become the all-powerful. The dust in the sky, in my lungs, was everywhere then.

****

I held onto the teddy bear and found myself overlooking traffic, all stopped of course, but it all led down to a tunnel right below me. A few people were passing here and there, and they all either looked completely scared and fidgety or sad and depressed. I think I was one of the fidgety ones, as I would constantly look over my shoulder at any sudden movements, even staring at the shadows, keeping my back far away from them. But, holding onto that teddy bear was what was calming me down a little bit at a time.

"Excuse me, Miss," a small boy asked, while he hugged a crying girl. Both kids, who looked around ten years old, had beautiful ebony skin and were dressed in a school uniform. The girl's hair was beautifully curly.

"Do you know where the hospital is?"

"I...I don't know," I looked up all around me twisting and turning.

"It's okay. We'll find our own way there." Both kids started walking away from me.

"No, wait!" I grabbed him by the shoulder and yanked him back.

"Ouch!" he cried out.

"Sorry." I put my hands up in the air. "Look, kids. I'm trying to find the hospital, too. Maybe we can work together and look for it." I smiled at them both, but the girl continued crying, and the boy looked at me quizzically.

"Are you sure you won't just leave us?" he asked me, as he tilted his head. "Because that's what someone else said, and they left, too."

"What? Who would leave two kids alone? Who would leave you two alone?"

"Well, we were running from something, and the two girls we were with helped us over a fence, and we ran behind a building. The two girls didn't follow us, so after a while I took a look, and there was just clothes and dirt, so they just left us alone."

"Well, I won't leave you two alone. Okay?" I smiled down at them. "Hey, little girl. What's your name?" She didn't answer, so I looked at the boy.

"Her name is Vira. She's my sister, and I'm Terry," he extended his arm outwards, but the entire time, he hadn't smiled. I shook his hand in greeting.

"Hey, Vira, sweetie. Can you look at me?" I looked over at the boy, and he just shrugged. "Do you like teddy bears, Vira?"

"She doesn't. She's a big nerd. She likes telescopes and...all the other scopes," her brother teased her.

"Am not," she shouted out with tears. "I do like teddy bears." She reached out to the one I was giving her, and she started to calm down, except for the occasional hiccup of a sob.

"Hey, look. Terry is smiling now," I said sweetly to them, and Terry quickly dropped his smile and tried to act melancholy again. Then, something dawned on me, as I looked closely at them. "Hey are you two twins?"

"Yeah, we're twins." Terry opened his mouth to interrupt before Vita continued. "Well, fraternal twins, and Terry here always tries to act like our dad, with a serious expression every time," Vira teased him, and he still remained gloomy but then stuck out his tongue at her.

We all shared a small laugh right then, and I turned around. "Okay, guys. I am going to need you both to follow me. Okay?" I led the way across the path overlooking the tunnel entrance. *The next person I see I will ask where the hospital is, and I'll keep asking until I finally get an answer.*

"Excuse me, sir. Where is the hospital?" I asked a bald man in a white long-sleeve shirt, with blood running down from his neckline to the bottom of the shirt and dry blood from his nose.

"I don't know," he mumbled out and kept walking. I turned to the kids and smiled at them and showed both my thumbs up. *I think I need them more than they need me.*

"Excuse me, ma'am," I asked an elderly woman going up a few steps and unlocking a door to a two-story house. "Where can we find the hospital?"

She looked at us three. "Oh, dear. I think the hospital is down Flower Lane. It's a side entrance. But, it should be just further up ahead and to the right...oh, don't take the first right. Take the second one." She smiled at us and slammed the door behind her. I turned around beaming a smile at them, feeling happier for myself.

"Well, she could have at least offered us water or something," Terry said pouting, while Vira giggled and held the teddy bear.

"Well, are you guys hungry?" I asked, starting to feel my stomach rumble.

"Well, no. But, I heard your stomach, so I guess you are," he said pointing to my stomach.

"Terry, that's not nice." Vira slapped his hand away and giggled again. "Oh, what's your name? We didn't ask."

"My name is Lupita, but you can both call me Lu," I smiled at them, as we continued walking. "So, why are you guys going to the hospital?"

"Our mom and dad work there," Terry answered. "Our dad is a security there, and Mom is a doctor."

"She is an obstetrician," Vira sounded every syllable as she said it and smiled as she wiped away her tears.

"We both don't know what that means though," Terry quickly interjected. "My sister may be smart, but she doesn't know half the words she studies." He laughed, as Vira made a mad face at him. I couldn't help but laugh, too.

"Are you laughing at me?" Vira looked so sad at me then.

"No, no sweetie. You're just too cute, and you have a beautiful face." I stopped and bent down to hug her. "I'm sorry. I won't laugh anymore." I looked at Terry with a stern face. "And you, young man you are going to have to behave and take care of your sister. Okay?"

Terry looked up at me, beaming a smile and started getting teary eyed. "That's what my dad always said to me." He quickly hugged me, and Vira soon joined the hug. I held them both tightly.

I wished that would have never ended. I wanted the warmth of a hug to go on forever. I wanted that hug to not be ruined, but the scream coming from behind us startled all of us. We all stood up stiffly, peering into the dusty veil, and suddenly, the earth rocked making us stumble.

"Run!" A man suddenly came running and holding a gun pointing it behind him.

"Come on, guys. Run!" I reached for both their hands, and we sprinted.

Gunshots continued ringing out, and we continued ducking. The earth continued shaking, and I knew something big was coming. *Don't turn around! Don't turn around!* I screamed in my mind. Off to my side, I could hear Vira start huffing and puffing and crying. Terry was gasping for air, but he kept on moving. Screams started to sound from in front of us, as we started passing a few groups of people. The earth continued shaking as we stumbled from left to right, and the gunshots still rang out.

"I need to stop," Vira shouted, as she almost tripped over a bent stop sign. We were zigzagging between cars and people, and I held on tightly to the kids, afraid they would lose me if something happened. *Come on! Come on! There has to be a way out!* I quickly scanned anyway that seemed possible, but almost everything seemed to be blocked with vehicles, fires, or collapsed buildings.

"Just keep running, okay. Just keep running!" I screamed out to them. We started to form a large group of people, running away from the stomping. I looked over ever so slightly, and I saw a woman's face distorted in absolute fear, with tears raining down and mixing in with her runny nose. She saw me looking and suddenly looked in front of her, her eyes wide open. I quickly looked in her direction and moved to the left, the only way that was available. There were so many screams behind that I just dared not look. *This is so scary. This is exactly what a nightmare is.*

Everyone around us all of a sudden fell as the ground shook roughly. The sides of the buildings and the windows broke and fell raining down, crashing and blowing up more dust. Everyone started to get to their feet and moved away, but the rest of us stayed down.

A few people started scrambling up over a few cars, and then "CRASH!" A giant stump of a foot crashed down on those few people on top of the car. I covered my head as I heard people screaming and screaming, and I felt a large wet droplet fall from above, and when it crashed in front of me and exploded outwards, every droplet that touched my skin burned. I cried out in pain, and I felt my insides starting to burn. I felt myself withering and screaming in pain.

Please! Oh, please! Just end it now! Tears streamed down my face, and I tried wiping away where the droplets hit me, but there was only blood coming out.

"Lupita, come on!" I don't know who yelled out my name, but whoever it was, was tugging on my legs, trying desperately to drag me away.

"PLEASE! OH, GOD! SOMEONE PLEASE HELP ME!" Every ounce of my body started to burn, and I started thrashing harder and harder, feeling my skull hit the pavement below with a loud SMACK.

"Lupita!" The voice rang out again. Other screams rang around, some intensifying and some dying down.

"Stop it, Lupita!" Right in my ear, a teary voice screamed out.

SMACK, my head hit the pavement. More screams rang out and more gunshots now.

BLAM BLAM BLAM!! Quick gunshots spread above us all.

"Get them out of here," a man's voice shouted!

"Please, just stop the pain." I begged to anyone.

SMACK! I could feel liquid come from my ears and nose.

"Lupita!" Then, I could hear the shout slowly fading away, along with everything else.

"No, let go of me!"

"Lupita! Help! Lupita!" I slowly started to lose hearing, but I started welcoming the darkness, the numbness.

"No!" I quickly shot up and coughed. I was half buried in the dust and covered in dry blood. Looking around, it was dark. Only the fires in the distance illuminated what was around me. "Terry! Vira!" I got up shaky and wobbly. "Terry! Vira!" I stumbled to a crushed car and leaned on it. Looking around, all I saw were mounds of dust and clothing everywhere.

Oh no! No! No! This can't be happening. "Vira!" A few feet from where I lay, I saw half the teddy bear sticking out. I quickly went for it, but stumbling down to the ground, I crawled through the dust.

I wanted to cry, but I was done with tears. I just sobbed without the waterworks. I was in pain everywhere. I just wanted to stop and sleep. I finally reached the teddy bear and held it tightly. I lay on my back, and for a little while, I stared at the dust swirl in the air. I ran my hands through the dust on the ground and pulled out a watch.

Without thinking, I started to dig through the dust and I pulled out a belt, shoes, and necklaces. *I know what this is now.* I felt my body shudder, but I remained laying on top of the dust. *This is the dust of the people. This is the dust of everyone, and I'm lying on them.*

I quickly turned to my side and crawled a few paces away from the mounds of dust and threw up. All that came out was saliva and small amounts of water. I lay there staring into the darkness, seeing the small flames in the distance dance around, engulfing cars and buildings.

I just stared. I didn't think. I just stared. The flames were going up and down, dying in some places and being brought back to life in other places. I stared at the dust just moving and swirling. I stared at the monsters that were crawling, walking, or flying everywhere in the darkness. Hiding in the shadows, they waited and watched for any movement, sniffing the air or straining to hear.

"Lupita," a hiss came from behind the car. *It's just my imagination,* I thought. That can't be real. I turned and saw Vira crouching in the darkness, her face slightly illuminated from the orange glow of the fire. "Lupita, is that you?" I cocked my head to the side and a small smile started forming.

"Vi…" I started to say out loud, but she interrupted me.

"Shh," she hissed again. "Stay quiet okay and follow me." She reached her hand over, and I took it.

"How did you not turn to dust?"

"What?" she whispered turning her face to me.

"I'll tell you later. Where is your brother?"

She smiled and continued leading me away from all the monsters and the mounds. Away from the chaos that had taken place not too long ago. I was glad, no happy and ecstatic that Vira was alive. I hoped the smile when I asked about her brother meant he was alive, too.

Going into an alley, I saw Terry holding a door open. I beamed a smile at him, as he smiled too, crying silently. He beckoned for us, and Vira, still holding my hand, quickly made our way to him. As soon as I got to the open doorway, I hugged them both.

"I'm so glad you're both alive right now," I whispered to both of them.

****

It was dark already, and I stayed near the sidewalk closer to the building. I was in a residential area, and I kept quiet most of the time. I knew there was more monsters out there. *How can there be something so...not real here.* It was possible, but there I was cowering in fear that they would find me and eat me or something.

I'm not sure people understood that just a few short hours ago people were thinking it was a terrorist attack. Then, they had to get through their heads that it was supernatural or something like that. *I don't even think it's going through my head at all. I know there are monsters...I know I am afraid.... But, everything feels off.*

I quickly ducked, as a monster steadily walked behind a car on the other side of me. Up ahead of me, the street was blocked by a few monsters, and right above, I heard a flapping noise. Looking up, I saw a few birds staring down at me. *Just some crows.* I peered, but they just looked like normal crows to me.

I moved further up ahead and heard the crows land where I used to be. Taking a quick peek, I saw two of the crows and looked back in front of me. *Okay, keep moving and avoid them.* I started staying away from people as well. I was tired of getting people hurt, and I wasn't going to do it anymore.

Crouching, I snuck over to the next car and the next and the next. *Everything seems to be going well.* I smiled, and right then, I knew I had spoken too soon. The crows pecked me, and when they touched my back, I felt a slight burn through my shirt.

"Ouch!" I fell forward and looked behind me. I could barely make out the crow, but it looked like its bones were poking out. My eyes wide with fear, I scrambled, and just as I got up right on top of the hood of the car, there was that same creature I had seen earlier, just smiling at me with all its sharp teeth.

I booked it, and I know I screamed. I ran and ran and ran. Small fires illuminated my way, and the crow monsters flying overhead swooped down, diving themselves at me like kamikaze fighters. Those that missed splattered onto the hard concrete right at my heels, killing themselves instantly.

I decided to stay close to the fires as they were the only way to see. They barely penetrated the thick dust though, so I had to quickly and cautiously run through my surroundings. *I'm lost,* quickly passed through my head, as I tried finding a way east. But, in the darkness and with fires around me, I was completely lost. I sprinted down an alley and saw three people huddled near an open doorway.

"Hey!" I shouted. "Help! Help me!" I saw it was a girl, who was maybe my age and two younger kids with her. And just behind me, I heard more splats as the crow beasts hit right behind me.

"Get inside. Come on, you guys." I heard the girl usher the two kids inside.

Afraid that they would close the door behind them and leave me trapped out there, I sprinted faster and faster. "Wait! Please, don't leave me out here." I saw the girl staring right behind me, and I heard heavy footsteps approaching fast.

"Hurry! Come on!" the girl yelled.

I was so close. I knew I could make it, and just then, I saw a large arm reach from my side, ready to swipe. I ducked and tripped. I rolled, and the creature tripped on me, too. I felt a searing burning pain, but ignoring it, I jumped on the thing's back and made it to the doorway, just as the girl slammed it shut.

"Who are you?" probed the girl. She had dark hair, still a bit wavy but also sticking out in every direction, and her face was very dusty with dry blood covering her arms and face.

I leaned down, trying to catch my breath, feeling the painful burning sensation slowly start to fade away. "I'm..." I was still gasping for breath, and I couldn't finish what I was saying. The two kids behind the girl seemed to be about ten or eleven years old. They were far too young to be part of the nightmare. "Johnny." I breathed out. "My name is Johnny." I slid to the ground and leaned forward, just as the door grew a dent. I scrambled to my feet. Everything was being illuminated by the fires, and a big metal grate with small holes everywhere let in an orange glow from outside. I could faintly hear the crackle of a fire on the other side.

BANG!!!

"They are going to get through!" screamed the little girl, cowering behind a teddy bear.

"We have to go now." The girl turned away from me and looked at the kids. "Terry, Vira, did you see another way out from here?"

"There is a front exit, but it has that metal giant door that you pull down," Terry answered quickly.

I looked around, and we were in a little kitchen with pizza signs everywhere. "I can help with that," I said, as we made our way to the front of the kitchen and over a counter. I looked around, and there were a few tables and chairs turned over and leftover pizza crust on the floor. In front of us, there was glass all over the floor, but someone had put the metal gate down.

"If they were able to put it down without electricity, I think it can be pulled up by hand," the girl said, starting to look for a lever at the side. Terry and Vira joined her, as I joined in the search.

BANG!

"Hurry, they are going to get through!"

BANG! BANG!

"I don't see it on the sides here!"

"Neither on here," I said panicking.

"I don't want to die in a pizza store," Terry shouted and started trying to lift the metal door. He reached down, and there was a lock with a key ring. We all looked at each other and scrambled back to the counter.

BANG! BANG! BANG!

"Hurry! Hurry!"

"I can't find it! I can't see it!" I screamed.

"Keep looking," the girl screamed. A sudden screeching sound came from behind us. I looked back and the bottom corner of the doorway was being pulled outward. Right away, I saw a hook above the light switch with a set of keys.

"Look," I shouted pointing at the hook. "It's right there, the keys!"

I stared at the girl, as she stared back at me. I could see her gulping, as I gulped as well. Then, the boy suddenly sprinted in front of us.

"Terry!" Both the girls screamed, as he quickly dashed forward, unhooked the keys, and jumping over the beast's swiping hand.

"You stupid, idiot," Vira shouted, as she hugged him when he got close.

The girl reached down and hugged him, too. "Don't do that again, okay. You scared us."

"Well, you were both just standing around." Just then, the screeching door was pulled apart more and more.

"Now, let's go! Come on, before they get in." And, as if it heard us, the beast pulled its arm out, taking half the doors, and in came two of the crow beasts. I could see them better. Their skulls were exposed, and they had hollow eyes, with claws on the ends of their wings.

"I'll get the door." Terry and Vira quickly ran towards the front.

"Is there anything to stop them," the girl shouted at me, as the door kept being pulled wider and wider. I scanned the area, and there didn't seem to be anything, just small appliances, except for a broom and a mop in the corner of the counters.

"There are mops and a broom." We quickly grabbed both and stood in a defense position near the counter.

"My name is Lupita," the girl quickly said, before the crows launched themselves at us.

Swinging the mop I had, *I wish I would have taken the bottom part off first.* I waved the heavy mop at one of the crows, trying to get across the counter. I beat at its back and continued hitting it, until another one appeared by its side. It flew up into the air, hitting the top counter and fell down. I again began beating it. Off to my side, I could hear the girl swinging the broom up in the air, and I saw a few of the crow beasts on the floor, desperately trying to get at our feet.

"Watch your feet," I shouted at Lupita. The door in front of us finally came apart as the beast on the hood stood there with saliva dropping to the ground, making a hissing noise as it hit the floor.

Lupita threw her broom at the beast. "Run!" she shouted and turned around to go over the counter.

I also threw the mop, but it barely brushed against the beast. I then turned around and did a double take and saw a set of lock keys on a trolley. Quickly grabbing the keys, I pushed the trolley at the beast, sending it as far as I could push it. With the flick of its hand, it sent the trolley to the wall, breaking it into pieces. The beasts were different than the one I had seen earlier. That one was tall, hunching its neck, so it could stand, and still, it had its knees bent. There was a set of horns on its head like a crown with tusks pointing downwards and scaly green skin. It snarled at me and lunged.

I had been standing in the corner, between the counter and the wall, and I quickly ducked as the horned beast threw itself. I scrambled to the opening beside the counter and felt another crow beast swoop down beside me. I ducked down again and ran to the others.

"None of them are the keys," Terry cried out.

"You're doing it wrong!" Vira screamed. "Hurry! Hurry!"

"Come on! Come on!" Lupita curled and uncurled her fingers, in a quick rhythm.

"I think these are them!" I pushed them into the hands of Terry. "Now, hurry! Open them!" I went over and reached under the metal grating, and Lupita followed the same, but on the other side.

"I got it!" shouted Terry, as he unhooked the lock and threw it behind him. The roar of the beast made me quickly pull the metal grating upwards with all my strength.

"Go!" I screamed, as everyone scrambled out through the door or over the broken window. I saw hands right away holding it for me, and I rolled under just as the metal door fell hard. The horned beast and the crow beasts launched themselves at the door, making it rattle and echo above the roaring fire across the street from us.

"Come, we have to get out of here," Lupita said urgently as she led the way.

I followed, relieved that I had someone to be with. *I'm not alone.* I slowly smiled and cried as I took the rear of the small group. We then began crouching and moving, crouching and moving, and staying hidden for a few minutes before we made sure the coast was clear. "Where are we going?" I whispered to Vira, who was in front of me, crouching behind a cab.

"To the hospital. Our parents work there, and Lupita said she needs to go there, too." She quietly whispered to me, "Do you need to go to the hospital?"

"I'm not sure. I'm looking for my dad. He's a scientist at the university." I quickly looked around. "I guess I'm a little lost, so maybe I can go with you guys to ask for help."

Vira smiled at me. "I can ask my dad if he can help you. He's a security guard at the hospital. Would that help?"

"Thank you, Vira." We moved to another car, and then, Lupita led us down an alley. "But, I think maybe your dad would want to spend some time with you. Don't worry about me though. I'm sure I will get some help from somewhere."

Lupita quietly gestured for all of us to go into a roundabout, leading to a small motel. There seemed to be no more light from the fires, so we had to feel our way, as she held the door open for us.

"Okay, what do we do here, Lupita?" I asked her, straining my eyes to see in the darkness.

"Well, we'll sleep here, and in the morning, when we can see, we'll get our bearings straight."

"Do we look for a room, or do we stay here?" Terry asked, moving his hand in front of us.

"Terry, put your hand down. We're all here in front of you." Vira waved her hand in front of us too, to try to move her brother's hand away.

I chuckled and moved my hand in front of them, too.

"What are you all doing?" Lupita asked us, also moving her hands in front as well.

"Just releasing some stress," I laughed a little and continued by everyone on turn. After a few minutes of some good smiles, we settled down a bit. "Okay, how about we move some of these couches and form a fort?"

"Yes, let's make a fort," beamed Terry.

"I want to make a fort, too," Vira chimed in.

"Well, a fort would be able to protect us. Should we stand guard or something?" Lupita asked the most important question.

"Okay, yes. I'll stand first guard, and I'll wake you up to take watch for the second one. Is that a good plan?" I asked through the darkness between us.

"How about we all make the fort quietly, and we all sleep in it?" Vira asked silently.

"I like her idea better," Terry whispered to all of us.

"Lupita?" I heard her turn her head and felt her hair brush against my face. "Is that okay?"

"Yes, I think I like that plan better, but remember guys, we have to be very quiet about this."

So, we got to work, whispering where things were and silently moving things around. At one point, someone tipped a side table and a bunch of magazines went fluttering down.

"Thank God that wasn't a vase or something like that," I said sounding tense. "Are there anymore tables around here?"

"I think we moved them all," Lupita hissed at me from behind something.

"I found some jackets we can use as blankets." Vira came crawling right in front of me.

"Are we all set for the fort," Terry asked excitedly.

"I think so," both Lupita and I said at the same time.

"Good, 'cause I am tired." Terry started moving towards my voice as well as two more sets of shuffling around me.

"Okay, everyone. Let's get some shut eye, and tomorrow, we..." I began as everyone was huddled close together.

"Tomorrow, we get you guys to your parents," beamed Lupita.

I could faintly hear Vira mumble, "Home sweet home," before we all remained quiet.

Reunited Above the Flames

My dream felt oddly strange yet familiar...

Why! Why did you leave me and mom! You were selfish when you decided to leave. You didn't even fight to stay with us. I hate you so much. It's so unfair.

The letter that I wrote... I remember writing it, but instead of my hands just days ago, it was written by smaller, younger hands. Tears fell down onto the paper, as I felt deep sadness...*What is this? This isn't what I wrote that last morning.* I slowly drifted off to sleep, with my thoughts losing the fight to think.

****

I slowly woke up stretching at first, lightly tapping the top of a couch. There was a bit of light peering through some couch cushions, blocking both ends of two big couches turned on their sides, so the backrest were on top of us.

What happened? I asked myself as I lowered my hand and felt a body beside me. I quickly jerked back and saw Vira and beside her Terry, and...and Johnny lying on the opposite side of him. *Oh, no. I thought it was a nightmare...I thought all of this was just a very bad dream.*

"Morning," Vira's small voice whispered right beside me.

"Hey there, sweetie." I curled and uncurled my hands. "How are you feeling?"

"I think I lost the teddy bear last night," she said sadly.

"Oh." I was surprised. I had forgotten about the teddy bear... Memories started surfacing. Memories that I knew could not be real, so I forced myself to think of something else.

"You're not mad at me, are you? I didn't mean to lose it," she started getting teary eyed.

"Oh no, no, no, sweetie. Vira, look at me." I grabbed her by the side of her face, and I smiled at her, looking at her face and hair. "I think you woke up with bad hair today."

Vira laughed out loud for just a split second, before she covered her mouth with both her hands. I giggled too, covering my mouth as well. "That's not very nice, Lu," she said happily after the laughter died down.

"But, I made you laugh right?"

"Yes, you did." She chuckled some more before closing her eyes. "Can we sleep a little longer? I am very tired."

I smiled at her and nodded my head. "Of course, Vira. I'll wake all of you in a bit. Okay?"

"Okay, Lu. We'll be ready," she trailed off and drifted back to sleep.

I silently crawled to an opening and looked at the outside. The air outside was still cloaked in dust, but inside there wasn't as much. I could make out the front glass entrance and a few more chairs and a registration counter. *Find some food,* flashed through my mind as my stomach rumbled angrily in agreement. Without making any noise, I moved the cushion out of the way and gently put it back in place.

Looking at our makeshift fort, if anyone where to go in there and see that, they'd think it was just a pile all thrown together. Which it was. We had made it as fast as we could in pitch darkness. I scurried to the registration counter and looked over some paperwork trying to see if they had a storage for food.

"Ah hah," I quietly said to myself. There was a map of the motel and right through the doors behind me led to a hallway with a kitchen, another room, and bathrooms. I steadily made my way through the door and down the hallway. *Just stay quiet and be cautious.* I mentally noted those thoughts over and over in my head. "Bingo." I smiled as I found the kitchen. I went to work, as I searched all the counters and what remained in the refrigerators.

****

I woke up and saw the two kids, Terry and Vira, who were lying down, sleeping peacefully. I figured they were siblings last night by the way they had been acting. I looked over to the other side but the girl, *What was her name...Oh, Lupita,* was gone.

"Oh, no," I whispered not trying to wake up the others, but it still woke them up anyway.

"What? What is it?" Terry wiped away the sleep from his eyes, and Vira looked around in a daze. "Where is Lu?"

"I don't know. She was here last night, but she's gone now."

"I think she went out a while ago," Vira piped in shyly.

"What?" I hissed. "We have to stick together." *I guess there goes my plan to stay away from people for fear of losing them.* "Let's go. We need to find her." No one asked questions or complained. We all got out of the fort and made our way out into the dusty lobby.

"Why is there dust in here, too? There wasn't an open window or door was there?" Vira looked around and spotted a pamphlet with maps.

"A map," shouted Terry, just as Vira went to go grab one.

"Shh," I told them. "Okay, guys. I don't think she would have gone outside. Let's check those bathrooms over there, then that door behind the counter."

"I'm not going into the guy's restroom," Vira stubbornly pointed out.

"Well, are you going to go in the girl's restroom alone?" her brother mocked her smiling.

"No, you're both coming with me," she frowned and remained silent.

"Alright, let's go." I walked hoping there were no monsters there, as we stealthily moved slowly and cautiously. We searched both restrooms only nodding our heads to each other when we found nothing, and we looked everywhere. I peered into every dark stall, as Terry or Vira would hold the door open, letting in as much light as possible. When we found nothing, we made our way back to the front and positioned ourselves behind the counter. When we were just about ready to turn the knob, we heard the door rattle, and we quickly scrambled away.

I grabbed the big book for registration, as the twins hid behind me. I figured I could throw the book at the monsters if it was them, and then, we could all make a run for it through the front doors. The door opened, and my hands raised the book, ready to throw it when Vira screamed.

"Stop! It's Lu! It's Lupita!" she yelled in delight.

"Wow!" Lupita dropped a few things she was holding and stared at us as we stared right back.

"What were you thinking?" I angrily asked. "The kids were worried you left them." I could see the kids look at me from the corner of my eyes.

"I just went to look for food," she sheepishly said.

"I thought we agreed to all go together anywhere at any time." I noticed I hadn't put the book down yet, so I lowered it, putting it back in its place.

"Food," Terry hungrily eyed what Lupita had in her arms.

"I'm starving," agreed Vira. "Can we eat now?"

I smiled. "Well, don't hog it all, Lupita." She smiled too and rolled her eyes.

"What are you all talking about? This is all for me." She laughed and then set the food down on a table.

"Let's dig in then." I brought over two more chairs and placed them around the other two chairs, facing the table. One was bigger than the rest, and Vira claimed that one, watching over us. We enjoyed ourselves with granola bars, juice cartons, and water bottles.

"Thank you for the food."

"Oh, yea. Thanks, Lu."

"Thank you, Lupita," I said smiling at her. "I didn't know how much I was starving until..." We all stopped and looked out the front entrance. A shadow started moving, peering in away from the doors.

"Time to leave now," Lupita hissed, and we all stuffed our pockets and followed her out the door where she had come from.

****

When I saw everyone enjoying their breakfast, I was starting to hope everything would be okay. Then, that shadow appeared. I took no chances. It was time to leave. I was only happy that we packed as much as we could into our pockets and hands.

"Guys, just keep following me. I saw an exit through the back. It'll be dark for a few seconds, but I'll get to the door to let in light." Suddenly, a crash came from where we left, and we hurried to the exit. I pulled open the door illuminating the exit, as we all followed through. Johnny was bringing up the rear. We were suddenly in a parking lot. "I don't know where to go," I said sheepishly.

"I do. I found this map, but I forgot to show it to you because you brought food." Vira held up the map guide in front of her.

"Yay. Good job, sis." Her brother patted her on the back.

I took the map thanking Vira and quickly opened it up, scanning the location we were at. "What's this motel called? Anyone?"

"I didn't catch the name," Johnny said. "But, maybe we should move away from here and at least try to find a street sign right?"

"Okay, let's go." I led the way, and I secretly hated that. I wished someone else would lead the way. *I don't want to be responsible for anyone getting hurt, but I am the leader on this. Well, the unspoken leader.*

I looked back every now and then, as we ducked behind a car. I am not even sure if there were any monsters, but I just wanted to be safe rather than sorry. "There, I found a street sign." I pulled open the map and looked for Loop Avenue. "This leads straight to the hospital."

"Wait! I know this street, four blocks ahead and to the right is the university. My dad is over there," Johnny said excitedly.

"We're going to see Mom and Dad!" Vira and Terry both were excited.

I looked at them with envy. The memories I had made me doubt what was real anymore. *Okay, Lupita. Calm yourself. Everything will be alright.*

"Let's go then, guys." I led the way again through the sidewalks, keeping close to the buildings and zigzagging through cars. We soon found more groups of people heading in our direction.

"Excuse me," Johnny asked two men carrying a woman between them. "Are you going to the hospital?"

"Yea, kid. We are." And they continued going their way. So, we made our way with them; it was safer in numbers. As we walked, Johnny and I let the kids walk between us, as we started passing rubble and bodies. Everywhere there was devastation. I knew Terry and Vira had to have walked through all of this, but they didn't have to see any more of it.

"So, how did you all meet?" Johnny asked us.

"Well," I began, *Wow, it's been forever. Well, it feels that way.* "Yesterday on a bridge, they asked for directions." I smiled and laughed inside. "And now, we're here. Walking to the same place."

"Where are you going again?" asked Terry.

"To the university. My dad is a scientist, and he works there."

"What if he went to find you?"

"Oh...I didn't really think of that." He stared dead ahead as we continued walking.

I saw his eyes. They weren't teary or showed sadness; they were just lost in thought. "I'm sure he is there, Johnny."

"Yeah, he's probably waiting for you right now," piped in Vira's voice.

"Thanks, guys." He smiled, but it didn't quite reach his eyes.

"What were you doing before this happened?" Vira questioned all of us.

"Well, I was with my brother in the car, and we were heading to my high school...my first day actually. I was very late, and he was very mad. I kept teasing him all day, and then, the light in the sky...and then, he wasn't there." I was looking down, and when I looked up, all of them were looking at me. "What? My brother went to go get help," I smiled.

"I am sure he is there waiting for you," Johnny smiled at me.

"Yeah," the twins said at the same time.

"We're not those types of twins." Terry said. "We don't say things at the same time."

"You wish we did." Vira gently nudged him on the shoulder. Then, she screamed as she tripped.

I looked down where she tripped, and there was a leg sticking out from under a slab of concrete. I quickly pulled her to her feet, and I saw Johnny step in front of the leg.

"Hey, you're alright see." I brushed the dirt from her knees and hands. "Just a little bloody, but you are tough. You've been through worse."

She smiled and laughed nervously. "That's a big understatement," which made Johnny and me laugh, too.

"I don't get it." Terry crossed his arms. "What does that mean?"

"What about you two, Terry and Vira? Where were you before this happened?"

"We were at school." I helped Vira over a crushed car, and she continued. "We didn't see any light in the sky, though it was our science class and it felt like..."

"It felt like an earthquake," Terry interrupted. "The ground shook, the lights went out and the roof came down." He looked down as he finished.

"It was scary," Vira continued. "Terry woke me, and it was pitch black. We had to feel around. I was scared, and he was scared." She looked at Terry as if preparing for him to argue, but he remained silent as we walked. "It was only us two. I don't remember if everyone else had left or not, but I remember we were learning about earthquakes. So when it happened, I ducked down. Then, I fainted. But then, I felt Terry's hand grab onto mine, and he led me away. We had to arch our backs and crawl at places because the ceiling had come down. I remember...I remember accidently grabbing onto someone's hair when I crawled." She gulped and had tears coming down.

"You don't have to talk, Vira. It's over now." I soothed her, as she nodded her head and remained silent. I looked over at Johnny, who looked back at me.

"Mom dropped us off in the morning...she told me to take care of Vira and...and she left to go work." Terry started crying. "I had to take care of her and..." He looked around as if he was in a daze. "My head hurts now." He held his head, and we stopped.

"Hey, hey there. Everything is going to be okay." Johnny squatted down to be eye level with him. "We're going to get you to your parents, and everything will be okay after that."

He nodded, and we again helped each other over cars. The two men and the woman had long ago left us, but we were already with a larger group of people all traveling down the road. I looked down at Vira. She was so small. *I'm only sorry she lost the teddy bear. I think that was helping her out a bit.* Then, she just swung her arms side to side, looking down at her feet. *She shouldn't have to see any of this.* I looked at her, and her eyes were red and puffy, but she wasn't crying. Like me, I think she was done crying. After everything that had happened, I think both of us wouldn't be crying anytime soon.

I looked at Terry as he held his head. *I think I know what he is going through.* I have been through that feeling. I know his memories are betraying him right now. *But, I don't want to ask.* I moved over to him and hugged him. He returned the hug, but it was halfhearted.

"I don't know what's happening right now," he whispered so only I could hear.

"Everything will be okay. Just believe what you feel, not what you remember and not what you see in front of you." I saw him look at his sister and start crying. Silent tears rolled down, and he hugged me tighter. "I don't think

I want to do that right now." He let go of me and moved over to walk with his sister. I stood back with Johnny, as we both looked at him every now and then, wincing as he held his head.

"I know what he's going through," Johnny said, as I quickly turned to look at him. "And I know that you also know that feeling." I stared at him and nodded, as he slightly smiled at me, too.

"You can't trust your memories now," I mumbled out.

"No. No, you can't," he sighed, and we kept walking.

****

All around us, there was chaos, and I was just tired of it. Lupita was hanging back with me as we kept an eye on the kids, but they started hanging back, so we were right on their heels. There was a huge crowd in front of us, and through the dust, only ark forms formed further up ahead, until there was a heavy smell of smoke everywhere.

"What's going on?" Lupita asked, as everyone started mumbling, asking the same thing.

"I don't know...no one is screaming and running, so there aren't any monsters." I smiled, but she looked at me and shook her head.

"That's not funny!" She looked away, but quickly looked back. "Should I go see what's going on?" Just then, like a wave, someone said something about a wall of fire, and everyone started saying that.

"There's a giant wall of fire."

"It just sprang up out of nowhere."

"There is no way around it."

"I think we have to go through the sewers."

"I heard the sewers are the only options. Should we go there?"

"But, it's dark and may be flooded, and there could be those monsters there."

"Monsters in the sewers?"

Then, panic started spreading, and I quickly pulled Lupita and the kids to the side and over the trunk of a car. I could see people start panicking and turning, bumping into people and causing them to do the same.

"Stop!" Someone up ahead in the thick of the dust yelled. "Don't panic. Just repeat this information. The way to the hospital is blocked. The street right before it is filled with burning cars, and it's spreading this way. We all have to turn back and find another way!" Some people started calmly walking away. Others ran away, and many others stood still arguing.

"There is no way around! The fire reaches all the way south to the end, and it doesn't stop! Hasn't anyone noticed that? The fires don't go out. They never go out!"

"It's true! You know what this is? It's judgment day." A relative groan spread throughout the crowd with some "shh" also following.

"Okay," Lupita said. "I think that's our cue to leave."

"Where are we going to go?" I asked.

She looked at me and the kids. Terry and Vira were already looking to the ground with sad faces already plastered there. "We're going to try to find a way through the fire."

The kids' eyes lit up, but I just gulped. *Should I find my own way around and leave them alone...or should I risk my life and help them? I haven't even spent a long time with them. I barely know them, but Lupita looks so familiar. Certain memories popped into my head earlier, and they were of her beautiful face, smiling and laughing. Then, a beautiful rosy red blush spread through her cheeks. I couldn't help to smile, but they weren't real memories. Just like all the other memories weren't real.*

"Well, Johnny?" Lupita looked at me, as she and the kids had their hands on top of each other's hands. "Are you with us?" she smiled such a beautiful smile.

"I'm in," I heard my voice say it out loud, but in my head I was saying, *I'm scared. I don't want to do it. I want to go home. Vira is right. My dad will find me.* But, I forced a smile and accepted what I said.

"Thank you." Terry hugged me, and Vira joined in.

"Of course, guys. We're all in this together." I hugged them tightly. My mind was changing sides. *I'm going to help them.* I put my hand in, as the twins followed mine. I felt a slight spark when I touched Lupita's hand, but it disappeared, as we raised our hands in the air.

"Let's go find Mom and Dad," Vira said, then quickly turned around. "And your brother, Lu. And get help to find your dad, Johnny."

We all smiled, and I noticed Lupita avoided eye contact, but we kept marching forward, even as people kept going back or arguing with one another. Luckily, it was just limited to arguing and not gunshots. I am sure at that point people had figured out it wasn't a terrorist attack. Personally, I thought it was supernatural, but I overheard some people mention aliens and secret science experiments at the university. *But, that's ridiculous. All they do is teach... Well, I actually don't know what they do.*

Soon, we could all feel the heat, and the thick heavy smoke start spreading everywhere. There was coughing all over, as we kept moving forward.

"Hey, kids. Turn back. There's a big fire up ahead," someone shouted at us, but we kept moving forward.

None of us talked as all four of us stood side by side, slowly losing visibility as the dark brown curtain turned to black toxic smoke, as we smelled the stench of garbage everywhere.

"There has to be..." Lupita began but started coughing. "There has to be a building we can go into and..."

"Look!' Vira yelled and pointed, as the roar of the fire finally reached our ears. "How are we going to get over that?"

"Let's move to the side. There has to be away around this," I shouted. *I hope they don't ask to go under through the sewers.* I was more worried about the beasts than getting my feet covered by human waste.

"I think we should hold hands," Terry shouted, and I felt our hands being linked together.

This is like last night when we couldn't see... Oh, no! Don't jinx it. I don't want any monsters. We started following alongside a building.

"Look, I found a crane," Lupita shouted, as we started to go around her and a big machinery thing stood up right in front of us.

"How do you know that?" I asked her.

"My brother used to work on one of these," she answered back. "We can get a better view from up there."

"Are you crazy? If we go up there and get a better view, the fire can spread by then and we'll be stuck up there 'til nightfall."

"Come. It'll be quick." She began climbing, and the twins did as well.

"Hold on. Hold on. This is too dangerous."

"Would you rather stay down here?"

"But, it's still too dangerous. What if...what if one of us falls?"

"What if one of us gets eaten by a monster down here?"

"You can't answer my question with a question," I yelled in frustration.

"Jeez! You two seem like a couple already," Terry interrupted.

"Can we move along now?" Vira poked Lupita's butt above her.

"Johnny, come on... Wait, are you scared of heights?"

"What? No, that's just dumb!" I huffed out.

She smiled at me. "Then, let's go." She started climbing higher and higher. Terry and Vira followed her, and all three soon disappeared up above the dust and smoke.

Okay, okay! I am not afraid of heights. I am not. I am not. I moved to the ladder railing and touched the cold metal that formed the bars of death. I gulped and started moving upwards. My palms grew sweatier, as I moved one bar at a time. I dared not think. I dared not look down. I dared not look side to side. My eyes were on the next bar and the next and the next and so on.

It started getting colder and colder, and the smoke only got thicker, but the dust got thinner. *This isn't too bad,* I said to myself, as I looked all around me and just saw the thick layer of dust below me, and the smoke soon thinning out, too. The sky was a nice blue with clouds passing by.

"Hey, look who decided to join us," shouted Terry a few feet above me.

"Hey, Johnny," Vira called out peering out from above.

"Vira, don't do that!" I shouted, and she quickly pulled herself closer to the ladders.

"Why did you do that?" she screamed.

"What's happening down there?" I heard Lupita's voice yell down to us.

"Vira almost fell," I yelled back.

"I did not," she cried out. "He's just scared I might fall."

"He's making me nervous now." Terry's voice shook.

"Johnny, stop it!'

"I don't understand why this is my fault!"

"Don't make me come down there!"

Imagining that, I quickly laughed. *Lupita somehow turning herself around to yell at us from all the way up there.*

"I think he lost it already!" Terry shouted.

"I'm not losing it. It's just funny imagining Lupita coming down here." I continued laughing, while also clinging to the ladders.

"Johnny! Do you want me to come down there?"

"No! No! I am good! Let's...let's just keep going now." I calmed down, and we slowly made our way up. I know everyone stayed closer to me as we moved, so I wouldn't freak out again. *I mean it's not like I did freak out. I just thought it was funny.*

"Look, there's that box thing where the operator drives." Vira pointed out.

"I don't think that's what it's called," Terry chimed in.

"Shut up," she answered back.

"Let's all get inside. Come on." Lupita was the first to arrive and open the doors. "Watch out! Dust is coming down!"

"Cover your eyes," Vira shouted. Afterwards, we all moved up ahead into the small cramped room.

"This is a bit uncomfortable." I smiled. Then, we all screamed as the whole cabin lurched to the side.

"Everyone, hold on!" Lupita yelled as the cabin lurched one more time, before a snapping sound began, and we fell.

I felt Terry grip my arm, and Vira gripped the seat. Lupita was holding onto the door and the handle right above. Everything seemed to slow down. Lupita's hair whipped upwards, and Vira's eyes remained shut the whole time. Terry had his eyes wide open, but he looked like a turtle trying to get his head into his body. All of that would have been funny if it wasn't for the circumstances that we were falling to our death. Then, we all lurched upwards, and the door swung open.

"Lupita!" I yelled at her, as the flames shot up below her. The crane had fallen, and we were right over the fire. The twins were crying and screaming in fear, and Lupita clung for her life. I reached over and grabbed her, and when I touched her, my head throbbed.

What is going on?

Lupita danced and danced, as the lights flickered back and forth and the music drummed in our ears. She was so beautiful, as she made these amazing moves that wowed the crowd, and people joined her. Our friends would come up to us and congratulate Lupita for her acceptance to the university she wanted. I smiled, but I felt it falter, and I left. I knew she would follow me. I know she cared about me enough to make sure I was okay. I went out into the balcony of the big house.

"Are you okay?"

"What do you think?"

She sighed and curled and uncurled her hands. "Listen, I know this is tough...do you want to go home?"

"And ruin the party for you? Nah." I smiled at her.

"I've been by your side for too long to know that, that smile is fake."

"Let's just go back to the party. Okay?" I rolled my eyes, as I turned around.

"No, I want to help you." She stubbornly said, grabbing my shoulder and turning me to look back at her.

"Just drop it." I started getting irritated.

"No, let me help. We can talk about it."

"I SAID JUST DROP IT!" I stormed out and dived into the music blaring at me. I was mad. I hated that day. It was the worst day of my life, and I didn't know why I even went. I went over to the drinks and poured myself some soda. Quick as a bat, one of my friends right by the drinks hid a bottle of alcohol in a bag he was carrying.

I walked over to him and smiled at him, "Spill it now." He grinned at me and took out the bottle. Pouring a bit into my drink, I grabbed the nozzle and made him fill it to the top.

"Whoa, whoa, buddy. I didn't want to share it." He laughed and left. I downed my drink as fast as I could, ignoring my stomach doing cartwheels. I had never had alcohol, and it tasted awful. I made eye contact with Lupita, as she was staring at me. I smiled, holding my cup in a salute. She shook her head sadly, and I smiled and turned to follow my friend. I knew he would get drunk enough to share later on.

After a while, when people started leaving, Lupita came up to me. "I want to go home now."

"Are you sure?" I smiled at her, breathing heavily. I am sure she could smell my breath, but I didn't care.

"Yes, now let's go." She reached into my pocket and grabbed the keys.

"No, I am driving. It's my car." I grabbed the keys from her.

"You are drunk. You can't drive us home."

"Watch me." I beamed at her, smiling and showing my teeth. I made my way out the door, focusing on one step, then the next, and then, the next. I bumped into the door, giggled and turned around. "Are you coming or not?"

"PULL ME UP! PULL ME UP!" Lupita screamed, as she held on for her life. "JOHNNY, PULL ME UP!"

I snapped out of the weird trance, and I felt my head throb slowly, like a pulse fading away. I leaned out and could feel the intense inferno under us and sweat started to form on my forehead.

"Reach for my hand." I strained to hold on and to lean out as far as I could.

"I don't want to let go." She held onto the door frame and started crying.

I looked back, and Terry and Vira were crying and huddled in the corner.

"Come on. Lupita! Reach for my hand!"

I could see her as she nodded her head and gulped, readying herself. Just then, the doorframe broke from the top hinge, and the whole cabin shook. Everyone screamed, and I'll admit so did I, but I had to get Lupita before she fell.

"Just give me your hands. I promise I won't lose you." I don't know why I chose those words. But, she nodded her head and braced herself, as she jumped, and I caught her hand. The whole cabin shook again, but I held on.

"Help me," she cried, and I couldn't hold on with one hand, so I braced my legs and with the sides and with both hands, I hauled her up. Terry and Vira held onto my shoulders and helped pull Lupita back into the cabin. We all hugged Lupita, as she trembled in our arms.

"I'm scared of heights now," she said softly, and we all broke out in laughter.

"That's uncalled for Lu." Vira wiped away tears and hugged her again.

"But, that was very funny." Terry smiled also wiping away tears.

The cabin started heating up very fast. "Let's get out of here." I stared all around us, trying to find a way out.

"The ladder we came up on is on fire down below," Lupita quietly said to all of us.

"Why not just go on top of the crane?" Terry said as he pointed.

"How will we get down?"

"We shimmy down," he responded.

"It's our only way down," Vira responded.

I shrugged and looked at Lupita. She shrugged, too. "We're going to have go outside. Are you okay with that?" She nodded yes. "Okay, let's go."

****

I still felt my body tremble after almost falling and feeling like I was going to catch on fire. I tuned out as Johnny talked to Terry and Vira and had them walk outside of the cabin. They crawled on all fours. He turned to me and talked to me, but I didn't hear a word. I just nodded and placed a smile, so he wouldn't worry.

He nodded in response and gently took my hand. I flinched in response, as I felt the memories when he touched me, as I was clinging to life. He backed away and nodded again. I made my way to the open door and began moving slowly. I was then directly on top of the crane. I gently lowered myself to crawl on all fours.

"Are you okay?" Vira called out from in front of me.

"Y-yes!" I shouted back. I didn't notice the wind was loud up there. And, we had to shout to hear. I also didn't notice the metal bars were burning that I was gripping and had my legs on. I winced as I inched my way forward. I didn't want to remove my hands, but I knew if I kept hanging on, I would have blisters.

Halfway across, the wind up there had blocked the smoke and dust, so we could see clear blue skies, and we were far away from the raging fires underneath us. I remember what the person had said, "The fires don't die. They don't." *That's strange, and I wanted to laugh at it and say it was stupid but nothing is following the right order here...wherever we are.* The crane started curving down at too steep an angle, and the twins were too afraid to keep moving forward.

"Okay, we have to keep moving forward," I shouted at them. "We can't go back. It's the only way, guys!"

"O-okay." Terry up front nodded, and he gently and slowly made his way down.

"Come on, sweetie. We're almost there. We can make it." I told Vira, as she cried but never let go of the metal between her hands. I lifted one hand to smooth away the hair. "Trust me, okay. Everything will be okay." She only nodded her head and continued her way down.

"Everything alright?" Johnny shouted from behind me.

"Yeah...we know each other. Don't we?" I waited for him to answer, but he never did and so, I kept moving forward.

We kept crawling and crawling. It felt like hours that we were on our hands and knees. But, I knew we were moving inch by inch. All of us were completely scared then. *It wasn't because of the monsters. It was because...of me. I pushed everyone to go up with me. I led everyone to their death if there is no way down.*

"Look! Look!" Terry shouted excitedly. "It's the hospital! The crane fell on top of the hospital." He excitedly continued moving faster.

"Careful!" I shrieked. I was afraid he would slip, but he slowed down, and I could see him nod his head.

"The dust is coming up ahead!" Vira shouted. "What if it ends before it gets to the hospital?"

"We'll find a way. I promise." Johnny ripped the words right out of my mouth. Johnny, the boy who I knew, the boy who I secretly hated for some reason, yet I felt drawn to him, not in a romantic way, but a deep friendship. I felt as if I had known him for a long time, and when he touched me, I saw those memories... him drinking...my brother in the hospital...my mother holding me...other memories started mixing in, and I was afraid that I was going crazy. Or if these memories were real and this...this world I am in is fake...I looked down and was starting to wonder. *If I fall, will I wake up from this nightmare? Will I be home yesterday morning, or will I be home in the memories...I wonder?*

"Lupita! Don't give up. Just keep going," Johnny shouted.

I began my slow decent onto the dust, but I had a strong feeling that told me everything was going to be okay when we got to the end.

Going under the dust felt like going down into the horrors of what was hiding and waiting in the shadows. I was ready for the crow beasts, ready for the giant one that almost killed me, and I was ready for my death. I think I finally accepted it because deep down I knew it was not real. I know my brother would not be in the hospital waiting for me. I know I had given up. I bumped into Vira right in front of me.

"Why did you stop?"

"It's Terry. He's the one that stopped first."

"Terry, are you okay?" Johnny again stole the words I was going to say.

"Yes. I... I think it ends here." Terry sounded scared.

"Is there a rope?" his sister nudged him.

"Any cables going down?" I asked before Johnny could say it. He didn't reply, and I looked over Vira's shoulder. "Terry? Is everything alright?"

"What's going on, Lupita?"

"I don't know; he just stopped."

"Terry? Hey little brother. Are... are you okay?" Vira slowly nudged her brother again.

"Lupita, I'm scared. He's...he's just staying still."

"Terry, hey buddy. Talk to us. Is every..." Suddenly, Vira screamed at the top of her lungs, and I saw where Terry used to be- he wasn't.

"TERRY! TERRY!" Vira screamed and screamed.

"Where did he go? Where did he go?" Johnny shouted behind me.

I trembled. My whole body shook... *He's gone. He's gone and...and it's all my fault.*

Home

Vira continued screaming, and Lupita stayed in a trance, just clinging to the metal under her. Her knuckles were turning white, and her veins were popping up all over her arms.

"Lupita!" I shouted. "Lupita!" Over and over, I shouted, but she wouldn't turn. *She's in shock, I think.* "Vira! Stay calm, okay. Just stay calm!" She continued screaming and started crawling forward almost as if she was...*Oh, God!* "No!"

I quickly tried to move over to Lupita, but when she felt me beside her, she screamed too and pushed me. In a matter of seconds, I felt my grip loosen. I felt my whole body weight fall to my right, and I saw Lupita's eyes widen in horror, as her hands shot out but missed. I felt the dust enclose itself around me, as I felt my arms whirling around me.

I am sorry, Lupita. I am sorry, Terry and Vira. I am sorry, Dad... My head throbbed, and I feared it would be the last time it would hurt like that.

Dear Dad,

I'm sorry. This is probably the hundredth time I've written this, but I need to get this perfect.

I never knew you. You know that, or I hope you do. I never knew you, and you never knew me, and that makes me so angry. Why! Why did you leave me and Mom! You were selfish when you decided to leave. You didn't even fight to stay with us. I hate you so much. It's so unfair.

Why didn't you fight? I heard the doctors tell you that in your ear. I heard Mom and Grandpa and Grandma. Did you not love us enough to fight against it?

There is so much I wished we could have done together. So many things you missed out on. Well, you missed out on a great son. Mom cries every time she sees me. She says I remind her of you.

Mom says she still loves you. She said she'll never forget about you. But, I barely knew you. I was too young, and Mom is sad all the time. When we get in fights, she clears her throat and she says she's sorry I missed out on you. "What a great man," she says. But I never knew you.

I never knew you.

I'm only writing this because I have to. I'm going to leave this on your headstone.

From, Johnny.

Goodbye

"Are you okay?" Terry, Vira, and Lupita all stared down at me. I quickly sat up and coughed, gasping for air.

"There. There. Just try to breath, sweetie. Just try to get air into your lungs." A woman's soothing voice relaxed me, as she rubbed my back.

"You had a pretty bad fall, but you're okay now." I looked around, and we were on top of a roof...*the hospital that was below us when we were above the dust.*

"What?" I had trouble speaking, as I felt a sharp pain in my chest "What...?"

"Don't try to talk. Okay, sweetie. What's his name?" she asked the others, and Terry and Vira both said, "Johnny."

"Alright, Johnny. We don't have an x-ray running yet, but we can see what the problem is. We still have doctors, so don't you worry." She helped me to my feet, and the others moved out of the way.

"Can one of you help him on the other side?" Lupita came up beside me and put her arm underneath mine. I looked over at her, but she kept her eyes staring straight ahead.

"I'm sorry." I heard her whisper, and they helped me up a few steps onto a balcony that had a helicopter; then, away we went into a dark entryway. After so many flights of steps, I dozed off.

"Hey, Johnny." I felt someone gently shake me then whisper in my ear, "Johnny, wake up."

"No, just a little more sleep, please." I begged, as I turned over, only to wince in pain.

"Well, that's what you get for not getting up," Lupita said grinning from ear to ear.

"What happened?" I rubbed the sleep from my eyes. *Please, please, say I was in an accident, and I'm in this hospital alive, and there are no monsters outside, and there is no dust of the dead floating around.*

She looked me in the eye, and her smile faded, "You fell from the crane...it was about a good ten feet but...you are alive."

"To good to be true," I mumbled.

"What?"

"Hmm? Oh, nothing. Where are the twins?"

"Terry and Vira are just outside the door." She stood up and opened the door. "Come on in, guys."

"Johnny!" Vira yelped, as she ran to hug me. The air was knocked out of me because she hugged me too tightly. Then, she backed away.

"Sorry about that," she said shyly.

"It's okay, Vira. Come on up." She smiled and scrambled onto the bed. I then noticed she, Terry and Lupita were covered from head to toes with bandages.

As if sensing my thoughts, Terry said, "We look like we went to war..., but we won." He smiled as I grinned, and Vira and Lupita rolled their eyes. "By the way, I wanted to tell you that there was an easier way to jump where I was at. It was just a few feet from the crane. You didn't have to jump all the way from the back."

I rolled my eyes at him and groaned. "When did you get so bad at the timing?"

"Hey, I timed my jump right!" He laughed, as we all groaned.

I looked at Lupita, who sadly mouthed, "Sorry." I nodded my head and smiled.

"Did you two find your parents?" Both looked away and shook their heads no.

"Are they not here or...?" I didn't want to finish the thought. I didn't want to scare them.

"Actually, we were all waiting for you," Lupita said. "They wanted you to be there, too."

"Yeah, so we could ask our dad about helping you find your dad." Terry smiled at me.

I smiled back and looked at Lupita, pointing at her, but she smiled and shook her head, no, too. "Well, don't I have to be released or something?"

"Actually, they wanted you out of here once you opened your eyes. They said they need the bed for more patients." Vira got off the bed and walked closer to Lupita. "And, we don't want to be rude..."

"But, hurry and get up," Terry finished for her.

"Wow, guys. Calm down." Lupita frowned a little. "We've been through a lot all of us."

I shivered as thoughts of the light in the sky, the dust, the monsters, the crane, and the fall all popped up at once.

"No. No, I think now is the best time to go searching." I steadily got to my feet, and Lupita gave me my shoes and socks. "What? They didn't want to give me a gown?"

"They actually ran out of them along with a lot of other stuff..., but they have backup generators and plenty of propane and gas to run this place for what...?" She asked the kids, "Another two weeks right?"

Vira nodded, "If they remain at minimal...something."

"Something? Wow, sis. When did you not finish your smart talk?"

"When I know I'm already smarter than you!" Terry was left with his mouth gaping open.

I smiled and chuckled, as Vira left the room.

****

I was so scared when I pushed him off the crane. I was afraid those memories would come back, and so, I flinched and pushed him. I had no idea he would fall, but as he did fall, I stretched my hands out as far as I could, but it was too late. I saw him disappear under the dust; then, I closed my eyes for a few seconds. I heard a thud.

Then, Vira and I heard Terry's voice shouting at us from below where he jumped. When I saw him lying there in the bed though, I honestly thought I killed him when I pushed him over. I was afraid I was never going to see him again, but we watched over him as the nurse and doctors helped him. They said we were some of the few kids they had seen throughout the city.

I offered the twins to go with them to find their parents, but they insisted we wait for Johnny, and I was glad we did. While they waited outside, I went over and touched Johnny's hand...so many memories came flooding back. I understood everything then..., but it wasn't my place to tell anyone what I knew.

"Hey, is everyone ready?" I asked, as Johnny came out of the restroom.

"Well, it doesn't flush, but I think I wasn't the first to figure that out," he said as he high fived Terry. Vira and I both said, "Eww" in unison.

"Can we just get a move on?" Vira said holding her nose in disgust.

I knew then what Johnny and I had been doing. Even without thinking it, he and I have been distracting the twins from the horrors and maybe ourselves, too. We've been making these small games and jokes to forget the monsters and the… *No, don't think about it now.*

"Well," I clapped my hands. "Who's ready to go down flights of stairs?" I smiled at the groans from everyone.

We started walking down the stairs anyway, and no one argued. We did have to wait in line though because everyone was using the stairs. There was security and other people with golden stickers shaped like police badges helping people go from one place to the other, directing traffic or stopping people from going into certain rooms.

"Do you see him, Vira? Do you see Dad?"

"No, I don't," Vira said, standing right next to her brother, as they both eagerly looked at each security guard.

"Excuse me," I asked one of the guards. "Do you know…"

"Keep moving, kids. If you want information, that'll be the first floor, and you'll need a badge to get in." He continued moving along the people, and soon, we lost track of him and were headed down the flight of stairs.

"Do you think they are here, Lu?" Vira gently tugged on my shirt. "Do you think they are…"

"No, sweetie. They are looking for you. Maybe, they think you're safe, and so they have to do their duty and help these people." I gulped, hoping it was true.

I turned to look at all of them. "Let's just get to the first floor and ask for help there. Is that a better plan?"

Everyone nodded in agreement, so we made our way down the stairs. A few times, the lights flickered, and I would grip the railings as tightly as I could, expecting something to appear from the shadows at any moment.

"Everything alright there, Lu?" Johnny used my nickname, and it felt weird somehow. I turned around, and he smiled at me, and I smiled back nodding a yes.

When we did finally reach the bottom doors and had opened them, we were met by a stampede of people pushing their way to the front of the registration, all asking for the same thing.

"Have you seen my daughter? She's six years old. She was wearing pink tennis shoes."

"My father is sixty years old, and he forgets a lot of things, but he remembers the hospital. He always ends up here."

"What do you mean he didn't make it? He was fine just the other day, wasn't he?"

Everyone yelled at once and crowded the entire desk, front and back, as they formed a semi-circle. I looked at

Vira and Terry, ready to tell them that it was going to take a while when I saw they had huge smiles. I followed their gaze and saw a woman who looked just like Vira, holding a crying baby while the baby's mother had her head bandaged.

"Is that her?" I asked them, but they didn't say a word. I looked up to meet Johnny's eyes, and I pointed to where the twins were looking. He smiled and bent over to be eye level with the kids.

"Is that her?" Again, they didn't say anything but just smiled and stared.

"Terry! Vira!" A man's deep voice sounded from behind. We all turned around, and there was a man in a security guard uniform, with tears rolling down his eyes. I saw out of the corner of my eye their mother turn in our direction when she heard their names. Quickly giving the baby to someone else, she ran. Both parents ran from opposite ends of the room through a crowd of people. Finally, both arriving at the same time, they got to their knees or crouched and held their kids.

"Oh, my babies. My beautiful, beautiful babies," their mother cooed, holding them and stroking their faces.

Vira was crying and couldn't talk, and Terry just looked at me, then Johnny, smiling like he was the happiest person in the world, and he *was* the happiest person in the world. He hugged his father, and they all held each other crying and hugging.

They whole reunion grabbed the attention of everyone in the lobby, and everyone remained silent, as the family was reunited. There were many faces of both deep grief and deep hope, as they saw a miracle transform in front of their eyes. Slowly, everyone started giving them their space, as Terry and Vira's mom and dad led them somewhere private.

"I'm glad they found their parents. They are finally home!" I wiped away a tear that escaped its prison. *I thought we said we were never going to cry again...* I giggled, and Johnny looked at me. *I guess I never did keep that promise anyway.*

"It's good to see hope right now. For everyone." He smiled.

Terry broke away from his parents and ran over to us. "Come on, guys." He grabbed both our hands and led us to his parents.

The Truth

"Terry and Vira both said you two helped them all the way from the west side of the city," Abraham, their father, said to us. "But, how did you get across the fire? You would have had to go around through the skyscrapers or the underground parking garage."

I looked at Johnny and opened my eyes widely. I think he knew what I was thinking. *Should we tell them?* But, the twins beat us to it.

"No, there was an entrance," Vira shook her head, and Terry agreed.

"Yeah, it wasn't too hard. We just went right though."

"Mmhmm," their mother, Violet said. "You can tell us all about it later."

"I don't want to talk about the monsters, though," Vira trembled and hugged herself.

"Yeah, let's not talk about them," Terry agreed.

"What monsters? Like men in masks or animals?" Abraham asked. The four of us stared at him and then their mother, as she had the same confused look on her face.

"There are monsters out there," I said pointing to a window that showed the dust sky. Both just kept looking at us as if were joking around, and I wasn't going to waste a breath trying to explain to them the horrible nightmares we had to go though.

"Dad?" Vira tugged at his pants. "We were wondering if you two can help them find their families."

"Of course, we can try," Violet answered. "Are they in the hospital?"

"Well, Lupita's brother..." Johnny began before I quickly interrupted him.

"We need some help to get to the university. Johnny's dad is a scientist there, and we were wondering if there was a way to get there?" From the corner of my eye, I saw Johnny stare at me, as well as Vira and Terry.

"Well, we can try." Abraham scratched his head. "But, you will have to understand that I'm not just about to leave my kids and all these people to go out there. I'm sorry, but I just got my kids back."

"Oh no, sir. We understand perfectly. We were just wondering if there was a way we could get there quickly."

Abraham scratched the back of his head and then grinned. "I think I may have someone who can help."

I looked at Johnny, who was just smiling. Not grinning from ear to ear or excited, he was just casually smiling accepting that there was a way to see his father. After a while and when the sun was far to the west, we waited at the rooftop with the twins and their mom, as the helicopter's whirling rotor blades sliced the air, slowly picking up speed.

"We're going to miss you guys," I shouted.

"You're coming back right? That was the plan," Violet shouted close to Johnny and my ears. "When this is all over, I want you two and your family to come have dinner with us." She smiled and hugged us both, as we nodded smiling, too. But when we bent down to look at the twins, they were crying.

"What's wrong, guys?" I asked. "Aren't you happy you finally have us out of your hair?" I made them smile, and Vira rolled her eyes at me. She beckoned for me to come closer to her, and she told me something that made me tear up. She began crying and quickly hugged me and Johnny, before turning to hug her mother.

"She's just sad you two have to go, but Dan is our best pilot. We just have to take care of him, too. He's been through a lot as well, but don't worry. When this all blows over, we'll see you all soon." She smiled, and she glowed like an angel, while hugging Vira.

Terry came up to us and hugged us one at a time, and Johnny told him something in his ear. I only heard pieces of it, but I would ask Johnny later what he said.

"Okay." Abraham came from the helicopter bending over. "He's ready now. He wants to leave ASAP, before the sun sets, but it shouldn't take too long. He says he knows where the helipad is by heart at the university, so if there is anything covering it, he should be good... just be careful you two." He smiled and brought us closer, so he could say something in both our ears. "Just know our home is your home, too. Thank you very much for reuniting our family. I'm glad you both kept running smoothly through this mess. It must have been quite a journey, especially the light in the sky, but all we have to do now is wait 'til after the dust settles." He winked at us and hugged us closely, before pointing to the open hatch.

We made our way there and climbed in. Abraham helped us buckle up and gave us the thumbs up before closing the door and going to stand with his family. We all waved as we lifted from the ground. They soon disappeared.

****

"Hey, Dan. How long have you been flying?" I asked, as Lupita kept staring at me curiously. I smiled as Dan looked back and answered.

"Well, about four years now, but trust me, I am an expert on this." He chuckled and looked on ahead.

"So?" Lupita asked. "What did you tell Terry?"

I looked at her and smiled, shaking my head. *I think she knows anyways, but I need to make sure my dad is there. I have to see him.* "It doesn't matter now," I answered.

"So...what's your dad's name?" She asked as she looked out the window.

"His name is Albert. Dr. Albert Root."

"She looked at me strangely, "Your last name is Root? That's kind of weird."

I laughed at her reaction. "Yes, my name is Johnny Root. What is yours?"

"My name is Lupita Lopez." She reached her hand over. "Nice to meet you." I laughed and shook her hand.

"I see it!" Dan yelled. "It's there just under the dust, but I am sure it is there," he yelled.

Lupita still held onto my hand. "Are you ready for this?"

I nodded my head and agreed. "I'm ready."

"Alright, kids. We're landing.... Wait a minute..." Dan started panicking. We kept getting lower and lower.

I looked at Lupita, and she looked at me. Frowning, I asked Dan, "Hey, is everything alright? Shouldn't we be there by now?" We kept going lower and lower; there didn't seem to be a bottom.

"I...I don't know. It should be here already. The landing pad should be here!"

We peered out the window, and we were under the dust, so there was nothing we could see. I started panicking as well. *This is wrong! Something is very wrong! Where is the ground? Where is the university?*

"Look out!" Lupita yelled, as a building started coming down from above. He swerved from left to right, as debris started raining down. Pieces of buildings and cars and trucks started falling down. A giant roar sounded from above, and it shook the entire cabin even more.

"What's going?" Dan yelled. We both looked out the window, as we saw the city start falling from the edge. *I don't understand what's going on. None of this should be possible...well, none of this is possible anyway.*

"I'm pulling up, kids. We need to get out of here! Just hold on tight!" Just as he finished saying that, the motor blades struck something, as more debris fell around us, hitting the glass, shattering it here and there. "HOLD ON! HOLD ON!"

I held on tightly, as Dan pulled the helicopter up, spiraling upwards crazily. I could see Lupita clinging onto the sides and shutting her eyes tightly. A large clang hit the door, and it opened up, tearing away from the rest of the helicopter.

"Agh!" Lupita screamed and screamed, and I just held on. "We're going to die! We're going to die!"

"Lupita, hold on. Just..." The helicopter kept spiraling upwards, and Dan kept shouting. The whole cabin shook, and we went sideways, falling. Then, we were upwards again, going in circles and circles, as we got dizzy, and our heads snapped back and forth.

Somehow, we spiraled up way above the dust. In the distance, we could see the top of a few skyscrapers, and it was beautiful. The sun was setting in the distance, striking rays of orange and pink glows, with dark blue in the opposite. It looked so beautiful, and I shed a tear, just as I saw Lupita being ripped away from the cabin and out into the open sky.

"No! Lupita!" I reached out for her and then felt myself being ripped away. I felt the harness I was strapped to burn my skin as it released me. It scraped me hitting my sides forcefully. I tried hanging on, but I lost my grip, and I was airborne.

My eyes closed. I felt the roar of wind in my ears. *This is the end of me now. I didn't even get to say sorry to my dad...I am so sorry, Dad, wherever you are...rest in peace, Dad. I love you.* I felt the wind being knocked out of me, as hands wrapped round me. I looked around, and Lupita held onto me, hugging me from behind. Then, my head throbbed.

"Mom?"

"What is it, Johnny? Everything okay?"

"Why couldn't Dad stay with us? I heard everyone say to keep fighting...Why didn't he fight? Was he not strong enough?"

My mom bent down and wrapped her arms around my body, as I held a letter. It's been almost a few minutes as we held each other crying silently, and we slowly broke apart turning back towards the sun shining at us. We stood by his grave on that beautiful day. It seemed unfair that he was missing that day. That he was packed in the cold hard earth, while we stood upon him.

"It was his time to go. For some reason he had to go." She held on tightly, as she whispered in my ears.

"I want him to come back...I want to see him," I said.

****

"Johnny!" I yelled, frowning with anger. "Just give me the keys, and I'll drive us home."

"Lupita, it's my car, and I'm driving." He reached to open the door handle and missed.

"Hey!" He yelled at anyone outside, still waiting for a ride. "Last minute ride, right over here!" Three of our friends came over and got in the car, and then, he turned to me and smiled and winked.

"Whatever! Just drive then." *Against my better judgment. Lupita, what are you doing? Just go away.* "I'm getting in the back seat, though."

We both got in the car, and it took him a while to start it. Everyone cheered when he finally started the car.

"Yay, woo! Now, let's get home. Lupita!" He yelled from the front, as he turned on the radio blasting so loudly that we couldn't even hear each other think, with the music pounding in our ears.

I shook my head and crossed my arms. He started the car and pulled away quickly. I tried putting on my seatbelt, but it was stuck. Fast and furiously, I pulled and pulled, before I heard a snap and gave up.

****

I felt the steering wheel in my arms, but it felt numb as well. My foot started to push down on the gas pedal, and I felt myself get nervous; then, a cold sweat began. The music blared and the rest of our friends cheered me on, as they laughed. They started placing me at ease. I looked in the rearview mirror and adjusted it to look at Lupita. She stared out the window into the darkness.

I looked over to my right at the passenger seat, and I saw my friend scream and brace himself. I looked in the rearview mirror and met Lupita's wide eyes, full of fear and light. I quickly moved my eyes in front of me and saw big bright lights before.... nothing.

We continued falling, but we just stared at each other. We stared into each other's eyes, with red teary eyes.

I felt my chest throb. "Lupita, I am so sorry."

She nodded her head and smiled, "It's okay, Johnny. I'm sorry, too."

We looked below us and the dust started going away. It started settling down, and the city was in ruins, as it started falling over the edge. Feet by feet, everything started falling to the darkness, and without fear, we braced ourselves for the end.

"I'm so sorry, Lupita. I really am."

"I forgive you, Johnny."

About the Author

E. J. Astorga enjoys writing wherever he goes although the only problem is there are too many ideas forming in his head to fully grasp onto one, so he painstakingly concentrates until his thoughs form into one coherent idea. He enjoys the heat from the long summer days because he gets to stay indoors in a nice air-conditioned room and write his heart away.

E. J. immerses himself into his stories as well as other stories from his favorite authors to see how the world operates from these books.

E. J. is currently studying at College of the Desert and majoring in the medical field.